"I do see real truth in what you said," he told her, just inches away.

His gaze locked with hers as though he had some otherworldly, mesmerizing power. "But you are a beautiful woman, Christine. I'd notice you whether you were carrying my baby or not."

Notice her. Like he probably noticed most women of an appropriate age, as men did.

"Jamie..."

He held up a hand. "Don't worry, I'm not hitting on you. I'm just keeping it all out in the open, as you said."

He could have been hitting on her. They were alone in a deserted parking lot with the sun setting romantically behind them.

But he wasn't. She believed him. One hundred percent.

And that didn't stop her body from wishing that he had been.

That he could be.

That she could lean in and touch her lips to his.

But, of course, she didn't say so.

She wasn't going to get weak and blow this.

Too much was at stake.

Dear Reader,

"What if?" That's how this book started out. I'd read a story in the news about frozen embryos and my mind went on a journey of its own. We hear about women wanting children and going to sperm banks, but what if a man wanted to be a single parent? And then, being emotionally intense me, I had to take it even further. What if he wanted his own child with the wife he'd lost in an accident? They could have gone through fertility treatments before the accident and...

And Christine...she's had a cameo in a couple of books. Her story was brewing. I thought I knew her. And then she popped up on the page. I want this woman to be my best friend forever. She's everything I wish I was. Everything I try to be. Putting others first with honesty and pure willingness—not because she knows she should, or because she's decided she wants to, but just because it's who she is. I wasn't sure how to give such a woman a truly happy ending...but she showed me the way. It wasn't mine to give. It was already there. Because giving love brings love all on its own.

I hope you feel the love as this mother's secrets are finally brought to light.

I love to hear from readers! You can find me at www.tarataylorquinn.com.

Tara Taylor Quinn

A Mother's Secrets

TARA TAYLOR QUINN

HARLEQUIN
SPECIAL
EDITION

Recycling programs
for this product may
not exist in your area.

ISBN-13: 978-1-335-89467-0

A Mother's Secrets

Copyright © 2020 by TTQ Books LLC

This edition published by arrangement with Harlequin Books S.A.

For questions and comments about the quality of this book,
please contact us at CustomerService@Harlequin.com.

Harlequin Enterprises ULC
22 Adelaide St. West, 40th Floor
Toronto, Ontario M5H 4E3, Canada
www.Harlequin.com

Printed in U.S.A.

Having written over ninety novels, **Tara Taylor Quinn** is a *USA TODAY* bestselling author with more than seven million copies sold. She is known for delivering intense, emotional fiction. Tara is a past president of Romance Writers of America and is a seven-time RITA® Award finalist. She has also appeared on TV across the country, including *CBS Sunday Morning*. She supports the National Domestic Violence Hotline. If you need help, please contact 1-800-799-7233.

Books by Tara Taylor Quinn

Harlequin Special Edition

The Parent Portal

Having the Soldier's Baby
A Baby Affair
Her Motherhood Wish
A Mother's Secrets

The Daycare Chronicles

Her Lost and Found Baby
An Unexpected Christmas Baby
The Baby Arrangement

The Fortunes of Texas

Fortune's Christmas Baby

Visit the Author Profile page
at Harlequin.com for more titles.

For my mother, Agnes Mary Penny Gumser, who is the most giving, selfless person I've ever known. I learn from you every day. And I love you, always.

Chapter One

Okay, so we're doing this?

The definitive answer, a yes, came in the sound of ocean waves as Dr. Jamison Howe pounded out his morning jog on the beach. Sand sprayed. His tennis shoes thudded a regular rhythm in the thick substance, rubbing against the small toe on his left foot.

And in the sunrise, he saw Emily's grin, ear to ear, her eyes glinting with the happiness she'd never lost, even during the grueling brain surgeries she'd had to endure after her biking accident. She'd promised him, seconds before they'd put her under for that last surgery, that they were going to have their baby. Their family. She'd made him promise that

that's what he'd be thinking about while the surgeons worked on her.

The future. The baby they'd been trying so hard to conceive. It was going to happen, she'd told him. She'd been so certain that he'd really believed her. And had spent every second of those hours focused on a nonexistent baby. Imagining a boy or a girl. Playing with names. Picturing scenarios with a running or biking stroller, backpacks that held a little one.

Disneyland rides. Swimming lessons. He and Emily standing quietly, watching their baby sleep.

Which was why, when they'd told him she hadn't made it through the surgery, he hadn't believed them. Even after he'd been allowed in to see her lifeless body.

The truth had hit when he'd arrived home that night instead of sleeping in a recliner chair by her bedside at the hospital as they'd planned. When he'd climbed into their bed alone.

And he'd been bereft.

There was no baby. And no Emily, either.

Pounding feet. May sun half blinding him. Ocean breeze cooling his skin. Cloying humidity.

And still, *yes.*

Christine Elliott was not overly fond of exercise. It wasn't that she hated physical activity, it was just that most forms of regular daily exertion—running, bike riding, machine incline exercises, weight lifting—bored her. As the owner of a prominent, privately run fertility clinic, she was in tune with the need for good health. But she'd just allowed any other responsibility in her life to take priority over time at the gym. Or on the streets.

Until she'd discovered racquetball. Not as a sport or a game, but as a solitary physical expenditure of energy. She was up to five days a week, any week that would allow the time, alone in the little high-ceilinged room, banging the little rubber ball off the walls. Again and again. She'd upped her shot over the past year. Purposely hitting it so it would be impossible to return and then racing to return it. Sometimes succeeding, sometimes not. But always trying. Always upping the ante on what she expected of herself.

Always needing to prove that she could do more. Do better.

Yeah, she got that this was a character flaw: her inability to accept herself as she was. The incessant need to always prove her worth to herself. Surrounded by doctors—psychiatrists and gynecologists—and counselors at her job, she knew all of the rhetoric.

And there was nothing wrong with loving her solitary racquetball time.

Except when she failed to set her alarm and she ended up late for her Tuesday afternoon appointment.

That wasn't cool.

Nor was it completely true. The appointment existed, but she always built in extra time, and was only at her desk fifteen minutes before her four o'clock appointment was due to arrive, instead of the scheduled half hour.

Newly, though quickly, showered, and back in her tie-dyed sundress and heeled flip-flops, her shortish brown hair still slightly damp on the ends that curled up in the back, she opened the file on the top of her desk.

Dr. Jamison Howe. She remembered him and his wife, Emily. She'd attended high school with them, though, as they were both two years ahead of her, they didn't know her. She hadn't recognized them, either, when she'd met with them two years before. They'd been through all of the genetic testing, and while no apparent reason had presented for their inability to conceive, they'd wanted to speak with her about options offered through her clinic—The Parent Portal.

Reading the file, she instantly remembered details. The two, who'd been best friends since they were eight years old and too cute for words together, had decided to try in vitro fertilization after struggling with infertility. They'd gone through the embryonic process and had been due back into the clinic for implantation the day after Emily's bicycle accident. They'd chosen to freeze her embryos, for use as soon as she was deemed well enough to sustain a healthy pregnancy, but that hadn't happened. Emily Howe had died on the operating table the previous year.

The embryos had been in frozen storage ever since. Waiting to be destroyed, as was common practice in such situations.

Per the legal contract, between each of the Howes and The Parent Portal, Jamison was now sole owner of the embryos and the only person who could make that difficult decision.

A phone call, a notarized signature to the lab, would make that happen. He needn't visit The Parent Portal, but Christine wasn't all that surprised by the fact he'd requested to come in person. In the years she'd been in business, she'd come to understand the full emotional depths that people went through when dealing with their own fertility, their future. Most couldn't just destroy what, to them, once represented the beginning of their child, with a phone call. Some hung on to embryos for years. And while Christine had her degree in health management and was not a counselor, her clients often sought her out when they had difficult decisions in front of them.

She'd present the facts, most of which they already knew, in a way that allowed them to step back. She'd give them a glimpse of a fuller picture, one in which science and biology couldn't create people alone. Without the final component of a loving mother and a womb in which to grow, the embryos were just science and biology. Oftentimes she was able to help them see their way more clearly to a decision they'd probably already subconsciously made before they'd entered her office.

It was all part of the job she'd created for herself and taken on with her whole being. Her clients were all looking to create families of their own. The Parent Portal was her family. Her progeny. Her future. Her love and happiness.

Her purpose.

There'd been a time when she'd envisioned being a mother herself one day. But then an excruciating young love had put her on a completely different path.

A buzz from the reception desk interrupted her contemplation, letting her know that her client was on his way in and the knock on the door sounded a full five minutes before Jamison Howe was due.

She was ready. Had been in since six that morning to prepare for the day, as per her general routine.

She'd mentally chosen to conduct this meeting on the tan-colored leather sofa and chairs on the other end of her office. Something more comfortable and homey for what was sure to be an emotionally difficult conversation. There was nothing legal to discuss here.

Opening the door, she stepped back.

Jamison Howe, his thick, long, dark hair tipping the collar of his short-sleeved dress shirt, barely gave her a glance as he took seemingly purposeful steps right past her and lowered his tall athletic frame in one of the two leather chairs in front of her massive, light wood desk.

So much for homey and compassionate.

But that was fine.

Anything she could do to make this difficult time easier for him…

He looked completely different than she remembered. But when she looked back, mostly what she remembered from her one visit with the Howe couple was…Emily. The woman's unbounding joy in life. Her smile, which seemed completely genuine, from the inside out, even when discussing the possibility of failure of the in vitro process. The two-year-old impression of Jamison stored in Christine's brain was of a quiet man who seemed truly happy to give his wife whatever she wanted.

As she remembered, he'd been a PhD in math. Taught some kind of spatial art class at the local, privately run, but nationally known, art college in town. Also had a math professorship at a university in Mission Viejo, or LA. Someplace with a bit of a commute.

He'd had super short hair then, too, and wore dress pants with his shirt and tie, instead of the jeans his shirt was currently tucked into. He'd had a beard before, she remembered that. The clean-shaven look suited him, showed the strength in his jawbone as he flexed it.

Nervously?

The kindest thing she could do for him was get him through the next few minutes and out of there as quickly as possible. She had a notary on standby— an employee of the clinic—and they could fax the paperwork to the lab for him.

"Thank you for seeing me," Dr. Howe said before she'd even taken her seat behind her desk. "I'd like to say that I won't take up much of your time, but, if you can even consider indulging my request, that won't be the case."

She dropped a little heavily into her seat. A little less gracefully than usual.

"I have time," she said, meeting his dark-eyed gaze with the professional courtesy she offered everyone who stepped through her door.

The office was hers. The appointment, the need, was his.

He had her curious, though. What request could he possibly have of her? A notary took seconds. Faxes, the same. It was all standard procedure.

But not to him. For the father of the embryos under consideration, the choice he was about to make could seem like a matter of life and death.

Maybe he wanted her to talk to someone for him? She'd do whatever she could. Of course she would.

Her clients, every single one of them, even those she only knew by name, were dear to her.

Which was why she always tried to meet each of them, at least once.

"My request is quite unusual, and I've been rehearsing all day, in between summer session classes, trying to come up with the best way to break it to you. But if there is one, I've been unsuccessful in finding it."

Okay, so now she was really curious. The man seemed strangely energized. Not broken.

Sitting forward, her arms on her desk, she said, "Well then I suggest you just ask." Hoping that whatever it was, she could grant the request. The man was endearing. An unusual combination of vulnerable, strong, sexy and...a bit unsure?

"I've decided to use the embryos that Emily and I had frozen. To go forward with our plans to have a family."

She nodded, buying herself time while she assessed him. He seemed perfectly rational. Calm, even, as he made the statement.

"I take it you've given this a lot of thought."

"I have. For months. And I have no doubts. No hesitation."

She was getting that.

And absolutely hated to have to deliver her next piece of information. The Parent Portal was not a surrogacy clinic. They could do the fertilization process, would happily do so, once he found a surrogate, but they didn't hire women to have babies for others. She could refer him, though...

Searching her mind for the best option, she was already reaching for her drawer to pull out a brochure when he said, "You don't approve."

"My approval isn't even a consideration here," she quickly told him. "But for the record... I think I do approve, though I still don't like that word. More to the point, I think it might be a great choice for you."

Not for some, certainly, but perhaps for this man... "You and Emily...you've been a pair since you were in grade school." She said out loud what she'd just read again a few minutes before. "It seems fitting that you would continue on with what she so clearly wanted more than anything else...to have a child that was a part of both of you."

He nodded, cocking his head a bit as he seemed to assess her. Her words. "You get that," he eventually stated.

Her shrug was accompanied by a smile. "It'd be hard not to, even after having only spent that one hour with the two of you."

"Before that last surgery..." He broke off speaking, but didn't break eye contact. "She made me promise that I would believe that we were going to have our baby," he said. "For a while there, after she died, I was thinking she was just being her...you know...thinking of everyone else, of me...giving me something good to think about during surgery, but later, it dawned on me what she was really doing. She was, in her own way, begging me to continue on with our plans, whether she made it through the surgery or not."

The words brought her a second of unease.

"So...you're doing this for *her*," she said, careful to keep her tone even. Having a child to honor his dead wife was...perhaps...a self-sacrificing noble gesture. For the wife. But a baby...a child...a life...

"You're afraid I'm being selfish...thinking only of how badly I want this child...and trying to justify using Emily's embryo without her specific consent."

"Legally you have her consent, on that contract you both signed. Just as she had the sole and legal right to determine what would happen to your frozen specimen in the event of your death."

He frowned. "So, what's the problem?"

"Who said there was one?"

"Your tone of voice..."

So neutral hadn't been a good choice. Either that or the man was uncannily observant.

"I just wondered, though it's honestly none of my business, whether you were just doing this out of grief, and to honor Emily, as opposed to really wanting the child yourself. Like I said, none of my business...you have all legal rights to do as you've stated. But a child...that's a lifetime commitment.

And doing it alone…that's not easy. None of it's easy. It's hard. And messy. And frustrating. And…"

"It's standing by the crib alone, watching my child sleep," he said, his gaze direct. "Having to do all of the middle of the night feedings alone. All the baths. Mastering all the learning curves. Cheering him or her on alone, making all of the tough decisions alone. And it's bringing to life the miracle that will make life worth living," he said. "Trust me. No one wants a child more than I do," he said.

So maybe, back then, he hadn't just been happy to give his wife whatever she wanted. He'd been happy because he'd known they both wanted the exact same things.

For a second there, Christine envied him—the widower sitting across from her. At least he had a memory of knowing what that felt like—to have someone in your life who not only shared your hopes and dreams but really needed them, too.

Having been alone for most of her adult life, pursuing her career and what drove her, she could hardly imagine how great such a shared life would be.

"Okay, so I assume you're here to get the process started," she said, pulling out her bottom right hand drawer, reaching into the proper file for the pamphlet she needed. They were all there, clearly labeled, easily accessible. "Unfortunately, we don't provide surrogates here at The Parent Portal, but this would be my recommendation for a clinic that does. If you don't like At Home," she said, naming the clinic, "there are dozens of others in the state, and I'm sure one of them will work for you. Once you've chosen the surrogate, if you want us to oversee the fertilization process, on up through the birth, since that was Emily's wish, we'll be more than happy to do so." When he didn't immediately take the pamphlet, she slid it through the small pieces of three-dimensional art populating her desk to lay it in front of him.

He was nodding. Watching her. Pressed his lips together. Bit the lower one and then pressed them together again.

This was the emotion she'd expected when he'd first come in the door... Everyone reached that point differently.

She'd give him as long as he needed. Glanced at a multicolored porcelain horse, part of her collection, at her angel figurines, scattered in various spots on her desk, at a small metal heart-shaped sculpture...

"I've actually chosen the surrogate," Dr. Howe said, in an odd tone of voice that had gone suddenly scratchy sounding. "Or, at least, I know who I want her to be," he said. "She hasn't yet said she'd do it."

He met her gaze, but not as openly as he had before. Signaling clear discomfort.

"You need me to talk to her." She finally got what this meeting was about. He wanted her to talk his female choice into having his baby.

"No," he said, sitting back, both arms resting on

leather, his hands gripping the edges of the chair. His knuckles were white. She stared at them. At their whiteness, as though it was a signal to her, something vital.

"I don't need you to talk to her," he continued, paused.

"I need you to *be* her."

Chapter Two

"Excuse me?"

Jamie heard his cue, but was too busy fighting an unusual case of jitters to jump in with the explanation he'd mentally perfected over the past few months. The hard part was done. The part he'd found no good way to do—letting her know what he wanted to do.

The rest was supposed to flow smoothly.

And then, perhaps, maybe some nerves would come into play as he awaited her final response.

"I'm afraid you've misunderstood, Dr. Howe. I'm not for sale here. Nor is anyone else at this clinic. There are certified, viable clinics that help with surrogacy, but The Parent Portal isn't one of them."

The words should have stopped him. Propelled him out the door while uttering an abject apology.

They didn't. While her shock was evident, he heard no anger in her tone.

"You suggested surrogacy as a possible option down the road. When Emily and I met with you. You said that if it turned out that tests proved her uterus to be inhospitable, surrogacy would be a way for us to have the baby we wanted."

"It would have been. Still is," she amended, her expressive eyes wide and filled with compassion. "I'm sorry if I misled you, but I was only listing options, not in any way suggesting that I was available to perform them…"

He nodded. Remained in his chair as he'd started, leaned back, arms down. Mostly because he was a bit uncomfortable with the swarming in his stomach, the way just looking at her started a bit of a maelstrom inside him.

Emily had gotten emotional over everything. He'd always been the calm one.

So now that he was pinch-hitting on earth for both of them, he was suddenly going to be experiencing the emotions his wife would have, as well? The idea, while pleasant in some kind of bonding way, was not one he welcomed. Losing Emily had changed him irrevocably, to be sure, but some parts of himself had to remain as they'd been.

"I understand." He found his voice, because the

only other option was to sit there and let the idiocy tumble around inside him. "I fully understand," he assured her. "I was just hoping you'd hear me out."

"I don't see…"

"Please." He held her gaze steadily. He needed her to listen.

When she nodded, the odd sensations in his stomach settled.

"I'm not a fanciful man. I'm a mathematician. One who excels at and thrives on proving that everything lines up. And makes sense. There have been a series of events, starting way back when Emily and I were kids, that have all added up to this point. To my being here with you. I'm not about to sit here and tell you that she was some kind of psychic or angel on earth, or anything more than a human being just like you and me, but I can tell you that she'd look at me in a certain way, speak in a certain tone of voice, and whatever she said came to be. I don't think I realized it when she was alive, but since she's been gone, when I look back, I see that it was there."

"That's not all that uncommon." Christine's tone was filled with warmth, but also respect. She wasn't humoring him as many might have done. He wasn't at all surprised by that.

But that warmth in her gaze… It wasn't at all personal, but felt that way to him. His body reacted.

What in the hell was going on?

His life was a neat and clean spreadsheet. Not a

jumbled mass of inexplicable impressions. More than that, he honestly liked who he was.

"When one loses a loved one, the past becomes more concrete. It's a whole picture, not part of a moving and changing one. That life becomes finite to us."

He recognized the words. "You've been through grief counseling."

She didn't respond.

"When you have the completed picture you can study it more easily, and the mind naturally tries to make sense out of the things that stand out to us. For some people, the lucky ones, the mind succeeds."

She was throwing him off course. Yet, he couldn't argue her logic.

"Not to get too deep or heavy here, but I think that we all know more, deep down, than we consciously see," she continued as though they were there to discuss life after death.

Avoiding the real topic on the table?

He took encouragement from that.

Because if she was just going to turn him down, without consideration, there'd be no reason not to just get it done.

Right?

"So maybe that's why, after someone is gone, it's easier for us to see the places in her life where she was acting from that deeper place. Maybe it's those truths that stand out to us when we look at the whole picture that that life represented."

She was looking at the trinkets on her desk. And there were a lot of them. Colorful fake flowers in a colorful vase, too.

He got the distinct impression that he needed to rescue her. From this conversation, not from the flowers.

And that was bordering on him not being himself again. He was more recluse than rescuer.

"I first met Emily in the emergency room when we were eight," he said, off plan, but not completely. "She'd been bitten by a dog. I was there because my father was in kidney failure again. It wasn't my first time hanging out there by a long shot. I saw them bring her in. But I can also remember, to this day, her words as they wheeled her past me. 'Don't let them hurt the dog,' she said. Like I could do anything about any of it. Anyway, I kept walking by the cubicle where they'd taken her, and one time, the curtain around her was open. She asked me if I wanted to see her dog bite up close. Which, of course, as a kid, I did. She asked me if I wanted to be her friend, and I nodded. We got to talking, and when her mom came back from having used the bathroom, Emily announced that she and I were friends and her mom smiled and asked me my name, as though I belonged. I spent most of that afternoon in her little cubicle while they waited for whatever they were waiting for. When they finally came in to stitch her up, I got up to go and she asked me to stay. And when she was released and in the wheelchair on her way out, she told me to remember that we were friends. I remember thinking she was a bit goofy to think that we'd ever see each other again, but I liked the sentiment. I told her goodbye. And she said, 'See ya.'"

Not goodbye. "See ya." As though she'd known…

"A month later, when I went back to school, there she was, the new girl in our third grade class."

"What happened with your father?" Christine asked.

"I imagine he spent the night at the hospital, though I don't have specific memory of that. He most always did when he went into failure. He'd been in a bad car wreck before I was born. Both of his kidneys had ruptured. He had another transplant the year that I met Emily, but he died when I was in junior high."

"I'm sorry."

He shrugged off the sympathy. In some ways his childhood had been hard, with so much time spent in hospitals due to his dad being so sick, but in others, it had been the best. His mom and dad had always been there for him. Doing fun things with him. Giving him a solid base of love and security. His mom was still that. As was his stepfather, the man who'd been his father's best friend.

"Emily somehow knew we'd meet again," he said, getting the conversation back on track. "She knew that our friendship was real. And she took comfort from it that day, squeezing my hand and not crying at all as they stitched her up, letting me watch."

He'd almost cried, she'd hurt his hand so bad.

"I think she also knew, when she went into that surgery a year ago, that she wasn't going to make it. Or at the very least, she knew she had to provide for me in the event that she didn't make it. Her last words were a promise to me that our baby would be born. She made me promise that I believed her."

Christine's gaze narrowed. She swallowed.

But she seemed to have no calm and steady words of compassion to offer.

Dr. Jamison Howe was either one hell of a con man, or he was about the most unusual person she'd ever met.

He wasn't a scammer. There was no reason to con her. He could get what he wanted, a woman to carry his child, in any number of legally vetted health clinics across the state.

Which left *unusual*.

He was getting to her.

It was a first.

She had no idea what to do about it.

Except do what she did. Listen. Try to understand. To help. At the very least to empathize. To consider his suggestion fairly, compile the logical reasons she couldn't comply, and then move on with her day. To the next "Jamison Howe" or Emily Hannigan, a former classmate of Jamison's who had also been a client of The Parent Portal.

Life wasn't easy.

But it had moments of pure rightness. Of complete joy. Christine could attest to that.

She wanted him to have his child. Wanted to help him. Would help him. Once she got him past the whole "her carrying his baby" thing. It wasn't the first time she'd been asked. Was something she'd actually considered a few years back. But with her clinic, her position there, surrogacy had muddied her waters too much. There were a lot of great surrogates out there. She'd had clients at The Parent Portal who, after finding their own, had come to the clinic for the insemination, prenatal care and birth.

"I planned to give you a list of many such instances in my life with Emily, times when she'd say something and then it would come to be in one fashion or another, but there's only one that matters here," Dr. Howe said. The man was handsome from the hair on his head on down. His eyes. The deep timbre of his voice. The way he held his torso when he spoke—not upright straight, and yet seemingly straight. Relaxed, but no slouch…

"After we left here the day we met with you, she said that if it came to the last resort and we had to use a surrogate, it had to be you."

"She meant The Parent Portal, but I clearly misrepresented us to the two of you that day. We don't provide surrogates. I mean, we could. We just don't. I run a fertility clinic that insists on open family agreements, not a surrogacy clinic. I think it's best to specialize, and our specialty is not surrogacy."

"You told us you'd given your son up for adoption."

She stared at him. Had completely forgotten she'd told them. But now that he mentioned it… Emily had told her that she'd felt so strongly about using The Parent Portal because of the clinic's policy of acknowledging its patients and their needs, in the present and in the future. The woman had looked her in the eye, smiled and asked Christine if she'd ever had a child.

She hadn't prevaricated, even though she always did. But that day she hadn't. It was the first time since she gave her son up at seventeen that she hadn't. She'd told the Howes about the six-pound baby boy she'd loved so fiercely during his time inside her and then given to a family who'd desperately wanted a child of their own. Every day since, she'd been glad she made that choice, giving her son a family rather than bringing him into a home where his teenage mother was a nursemaid to her elderly grandparents.

"Emily said that we'd be doing you a favor by using you as our surrogate because it would help you to allow yourself to have another child."

He might as well have hit her on the head with a baseball bat.

It would have been kinder.

Chapter Three

Jamie wasn't all that surprised when Christine asked him to leave. The look of blank horror on her face had preceded her abrupt request.

He didn't blame her. As soon as he'd heard himself repeat what Emily had said to him over two years before, he'd known he'd made a huge mistake.

The personal remark, the reference to Christine's own child, had been totally out of line. Definitely not in his rehearsed rhetoric. But then nothing about the afternoon meeting had gone as he'd imagined it might.

At the door to her office, he turned, surprised at the tears he saw brimming in her eyes as she turned away from him. "I'm sorry," he said, knowing that there was no taking back what he'd said. "Emily and I had no business talking about you as if we knew you. And we really didn't, actually. Sit and talk about you, I mean. She just made that one statement and we moved on. I have no idea why it stuck with me. I certainly never meant to repeat it to you," he added. And when she didn't immediately remind him that he'd been uninvited from their meeting, he continued.

"I got carried off course, and absolutely didn't mean to imply that Emily was right in that particular assertion. Or to make you think that I think she was some kind of gifted seer who was always right. She wasn't. She was wrong a lot…" Like when she'd told him that buying their house was the absolute best thing for them to do. He was in the process of putting it on the market so that he could buy his way out of it and move on.

"I was only letting you know why I felt so strongly about asking you to be our surrogate. That statement from her is the only weigh-in on the matter I'm going to get from her."

Christine was sitting back in her chair, hands folded across a completely flat midsection. Ignoring him politely, freezing him out of there? Or listening?

"I'm certain about doing this, about having our family. I have no doubts or apprehensions at all. But finding a woman to carry Emily's child? How do I do that? How do I choose a woman to give birth to the child that my wife conceived and wanted more than anything on earth? It's not like I'm looking for someone to clean the house, here. Or bake my favorite cookies."

"You'd also be looking for someone to provide child care. Which you will presumably need to do after the baby is born as well. For now, you need a caretaker who's willing to do the job 24/7, internally."

His hand dropped from the doorknob.

She was engaging with him?

Should he still leave? Or was it appropriate for him to stay? Was there any chance she'd consider his request?

"Do you have a projected date for implantation in mind?" Her question had him leaning toward sticking around, but he didn't move away from the door.

"Soon," he said. "I have no date, no. I'd just like to get started on the process as soon as possible simply because I'm eager to have a family. I'm thirty-three," he ended, as though his age played some key role. It was Emily's biological clock that had mattered. Yeah, he'd like to be young enough to charge up hills with his offspring, but he expected to be able to do that for the next four decades, at the very least.

"I apologize for my abrupt response a few minutes ago, telling you to leave," she said. "I'm not used to people getting so intimately personal with me. At least not to my face," she said.

Was this really happening? She was coming around? "As I said, I was totally out of line."

Something in his stomach started to flop around again. Not a sensation he appreciated, nor one he'd tolerate once he had a moment or two to work on calming it. He'd definitely be adding some abdomen strengthening exercises to his daily regime.

"You *were* totally out of line with your personal comment regarding my life, and I'll forget it happened if you'll forgive my completely unprofessional response."

He turned to face her. "Done."

She nodded, picked up a pen and pulled a pad in front of her. "If you'll give me some parameters, I can get started seeking out candidates," she said. "This is nothing The Parent Portal has ever handled, as I said, but under the circumstances, I'd like to see if I can be of some assistance. You'll need your own lawyer, I know that much. And the surrogate will need a separate one. Rule number one in this state—whomever you choose, even if it's someone in your family, or someone you know privately, will have to have a full medical workup. The surrogacy clinics all have their own criteria, some based on state law, some based on their experience with successful matches and births."

"I've done the research," he told her, still stepping no closer to her. He didn't want her help finding a surrogate. He needed her to *be* the surrogate. There was no scientific or logical basis for his certainty on that. He just felt certain.

Could be the strain of pigheadedness in him.

Or it could be something more.

Jamie needed time to work on that one. For the time being, he'd accept what help she was willing to give him. Maybe she'd find someone who felt right for him. To him. Maybe.

He didn't think so.

"She has to have given birth before," he said then, to show her he'd really done research. "A lot of the clinics want her to have a child living at home, as it eases her ability to give one up, but I know that's not state mandated."

"It would be best for you if she's had a psychological workup, too," Christine said, holding her pen with a hand on each end as she watched him. She didn't offer him his seat back.

He didn't presume to take it.

The distance between them seemed…okay.

"You'll have a legally binding contract, but she still holds all the cards until that child is born, and you want to avoid as much chance of potential heartache as you can. The baby inside her might not be biologically hers, but her hormones will be working as though it was. You need her to be strong enough to love it for the time she carries it, and then let it go."

Yes. Exactly what he'd concluded. Christine got it. Her focus was on people—their emotional needs—

both those who'd been born and those who hadn't
yet. Those who wanted babies and those who were
giving them up. It was what made her clinic so different—the contracts she insisted on that allowed all
parties to seek out the others, within clearly stated
boundaries, in perpetuity.

He wanted her to carry his and Emily's baby. She
knew it all.

Was in great physical shape...

He gave himself a mental shake. He wasn't there
to assess her body. Before any embryo placement
could be made, a doctor would determine whether
or not she was physically a viable surrogacy candidate—assuming she agreed to his request, of course.

And that's as far as his knowledge of her body
had to go.

"So let's start with a list of what you'd like in a
surrogate," she said. "And what you have to offer
one."

"I'll pay whatever it takes." That had been a given
from the beginning. Not only did he make a good
clip, but he'd had a settlement from the insurance
company of the driver of the car that had hit Emily.
And he'd answer her questions because she seemed
to need to ask him, but he couldn't get past hoping
she'd have this baby herself. Emily having mentioned
her as a potential surrogate...it was as though on
some level she'd known...

"I wasn't just speaking financially," she said,

while making a note. "How do you perceive this going? How involved do you intend to be?"

"As involved as I *can* be."

"I'm assuming you want her to be local enough for regular checking in, then?"

He wanted "her" to be Christine. Right there in Marie Cove. Someone who wouldn't get creeped out if he stayed closely in touch, because she understood his situation. Because he was not yet ready to seriously consider an alternative surrogate, he kept the majority of his response to himself, other than a truthful, "Yes."

"Do you want to give her the option to pick her own doctor and clinic?"

Sure, if "she" was Christine. "No, I want the procedure and birth to be handled by The Parent Portal."

He got what she was doing, though. And appreciated her effort. She was seriously committing to helping him find the woman who'd bring his child into the world. Moving closer, he slowly retook the seat he'd vacated. She didn't even look up from the pad upon which she was writing.

"Any age requirement?"

"Thirty to thirty-three," he said, not getting too ballsy. "I want her more mature than twenties and yet still well before the thirty-five age bracket that some professionals say increases risk of problems."

"Do you have any marriage preferences?" Christine asked, looking up at him. "Some couples prefer married surrogates."

"I prefer her to not be married," he said, only because Christine wasn't. In his mind, Christine was it. There'd been no backup plan. How could he not have one, though?

He'd just been so carried away by all of the signs from Emily. The messages he knew he was getting from her.

How could he possibly have expected this woman to carry his child? Was he really that self-involved? Or so into the idea of Emily speaking to him that he was losing touch with reality?

Maybe he needed to go home and grieve some more. Get into the next stage of the process of living after your spouse wasn't.

He didn't feel like moping around. He'd miss Emily every day for the rest of his life, would always grieve for her, but he had to get out and start living life again. To create his new life. He'd been told that was the next stage. Had been assured by the grief counselor he'd seen that his drive to live, even though it meant doing so without Emily, was healthy.

And that, while it was a normal response for him to feel like an ass for having that drive, he wasn't one.

He noticed Christine studying him, those deep brown eyes seeming to touch him somehow, and it struck him that maybe this was what was meant to be. Perhaps Emily *was* leading him to Christine, not as their literal surrogate, but as the woman who helps him find her.

He wanted to think so but felt no conviction.

"If she doesn't live locally, but is willing to relocate to be close to the clinic during the duration of the process, would you be willing to provide a housing allowance?"

"Pay for an apartment, you mean?"

"Yes."

"I told you, money isn't an issue. I'll pay living expenses, whatever is necessary. The woman's putting her life on hold for me, allowing me to use her body…" He stopped when he heard how inappropriate that sounded. Instead, he wanted to tell Christine that he was willing to make a notable donation to The Parent Portal if she'd have his and Emily's baby for them, but didn't want to risk being evicted from her office a second time.

Chances were he wouldn't get a second forgiveness.

She wrote something. And then, pen slightly above the pad, sat there looking at it. Not reading, though. Her eyes weren't moving. It was more of a stare. Like she was deep in thought.

Introspection didn't usually present itself in the middle of business meetings. Unless… Was she considering…

Should he mention the clinic donation he would make?

Would that be tacky?

Or show her that he was willing to do whatever she needed to make their business deal a win-win for both of them?

What could he give her that would be comparable to what she'd be giving him?

"I'd be willing to consider some kind of arrangement whereby she could see the child now and then, if she wanted to do that. To have regular updates. Since, as you say, she will likely fall somewhat in love with the child as she carries it."

Christine blinked, as though coming back to a conscious awareness of where she was. Glanced at him and then jotted on the pad.

"I…please don't take this the wrong way…but I'll be making a donation to The Parent Portal. Not to pay for your help, but because I know, firsthand, how important it is that you're here. Thinking about this place, about those embryos… I think they might have saved me. Or at least helped speed up my recovery. What you do here… I just want you to know that it matters."

He heard himself and wasn't done. "Not to say that I won't pay for your help," he added. "Of course, I will. I intended to do so all along. I just…"

He'd turned into some kind of blabbering idiot.

The comic relief in one of the family dramas Emily used to love to watch.

She'd always been the one with the more obvious sense of humor. He was a numbers guy.

"You already made a donation. After Emily died."

He had, of course. But… "That was before I had the settlement," he said. "I intend to make another, and I should have just done it and kept my mouth shut. I just want you to know I'm a good guy. My intentions are pure and…"

Frowning, she put down her pen and glanced across at him. "I don't doubt your intentions, Dr. Howe."

"Jamie, please. We're in a medical clinic. The 'Dr.' seems a bit pretentious at the moment."

He had his students call him Jamie. Emily had been the only one who used Jamison. The way she'd said it… Like an endearment…

"Look—" he stood "—I bungled this. I'm not myself this morning. I don't normally ramble. Nor am I in the habit of offending people. I am, however, used to narrowing things down to the logical and then acting upon what's there. This isn't that."

"No, it's not." She remained in her seat as he walked toward the door. He had to go. Had to think. Maybe refigure.

"Would you just do me one favor?" he asked, as he turned to tell her thank you. And goodbye.

"I'll try." She'd placed her pad on top of a file. He assumed his and Emily's.

"Would you at least consider my original request? Let it just hang there for a day or so before dismissing it outright?"

It made no logical sense, his need to have her be the one to carry his child. And yet it was the only option that made sense to him at the moment.

Maybe after he met with the grief counselor he intended to call as soon as he was out the door, he'd see things differently.

Surely his emotional insistence that this near stranger was the only woman who could carry his child was merely residual grief. Something someone on the outside would see clearly. Nod his head about. Assure Jamie that he wasn't losing his mind.

Christine was staring at him again. He saw no horror in her expression. Wished she'd stand up and come out from behind her desk—anything that might make it feel like there wasn't an impenetrable gap between them.

"I don't want you to expect me to change my mind about carrying your child for you. Or even have hope that I might."

He heard the *but* she didn't say, which kept him standing there, tense and ready to feel the sunshine on his skin. To run until his feet burned.

"But, of course I'll let your request 'hang' for a

day or two. I expect it will be on my mind for years to come," she finished.

He didn't know if she was being sarcastic, or just plain honest, and didn't wait to find out.

With a nod, he fled.

Chapter Four

The roofers were still at it when Christine got home after six that evening. Two levels were done, the third, almost so. Then they'd just have the turret. And she'd get the final bill.

And was praying it didn't come in any higher than the estimate.

Old houses needed new roofs. And she needed this old house. She also needed money to replace the plumbing.

Still, looking at the new, lighter-colored shingles as she pulled slowly down the old, but statuesque street with its large, beautifully manicured green yards, she smiled. Gram and Gramps had to be smiling down from heaven. They'd loved this place as much as she did. Or close to it.

They, after all, had had each other—and her. She just had the house.

She knew she could get a loan to help to make the fixes. But the idea of borrowing frightened her.

When you only had yourself to count on, and you were your own employer, if something happened to you and you couldn't work, or your business got sued, you'd be unable to make large monthly payments, which could result in foreclosure.

You didn't put yourself at risk like that.

Her dad and her stepmother, Tammy, the woman her father had married not long enough after Christine's mother died, thought she should sell the place. But then they thought she'd been stupid to invest the entire inheritance left to her by her mother's life insurance to open a small fertility clinic rather than accepting any one of the high-paying jobs she'd been offered at a number of health facilities.

They'd said they wanted her close. Wanted their son, her half brother, Tyler, to grow up bonding with her. She loved Tyler's fifteen-year-old smart-ass self, but she'd never felt like a member of their family.

From day one, she'd been a mere visitor from her father's past life.

She'd been only ten when her mother had died at forty, attempting to give birth to a son who had also died, and her father had left her with her grandparents and moved to LA.

He'd moved on by becoming someone else.

Some people dealt with death that way.

Others, like Dr. Jamison Howe—Jamie, he'd told her to call him—moved forward, creating a different life that included who he'd been.

Was that why the man's request had hit her so deeply? Why his remark about her past had made her feel like lashing out and then wanting to retreat and be left alone?

Was he the antithesis of the man who'd hurt her so deeply, let her down so critically?

Was he asking her to help him do what she wished her father had found a way to do? Did he want her to help him take the man he'd been into the new life he must now create by using his wife's choice of surrogate?

The owner of the small roofing company she'd hired waved from the rooftop as she pulled into her drive and then around back to the three-car garage. Parking in her usual spot in front of door one, she noticed the peeling paint on all three garage doors and then thought again about the quote she'd had done to have automatic doors put in.

She just was loath to change the garage.

And hated to see it in disrepair, too.

She could borrow money from the trust that she'd designated for The Parent Portal—but while the clinic was currently supporting itself quite nicely, that trust money was the clinic's security. She couldn't put something she loved at risk.

Shrugging the problem aside, she gathered her brightly flowered leather bag—a knockoff she'd been excited to find at a street fair in LA—and made her way into the only home she'd ever really known via the back door.

It was her night to help out at the local women's center. She was teaching a class in crocheting baby hats, which would be sent to neonatal units overseas. It was something Gram used to do—and taught her to do—before the older woman's hands became so crippled by arthritis that she couldn't work the needle anymore.

And after class, she and Olivia, another friend and volunteer, were going out for a late supper and glass of wine. Who had time to think about a widower asking her to have his baby?

"It was just another day at the office," she told herself as she threw in a load of laundry, dusted the library slash Gramps's den, freshened up for her evening out—and said it again when she was facing Olivia over the booth they'd chosen in their favorite eatery in downtown Marie Cove.

"I hear all kinds of things," she continued, taking her second sip of wine in almost as many seconds. "Couples struggling to have babies are about the most emotional people in one of the most emotional situations. I never know what someone might do or say or suggest. By the time they get to me they're often feeling desperate."

In Jamison and Emily's case, there hadn't been anything making it impossible for them to get pregnant. They just hadn't conceived.

Olivia's dark-eyed gaze softened. "You want to tell me what's going on?" They'd both ordered grilled chicken ranch salads, which should have been there already and weren't. Christine looked around for their waitress.

Olivia insisted she was single because she just hadn't met the right man yet. Christina wasn't so sure. In the six years the woman had been her friend, she'd never known Olivia to have gone on any dates. Though she had a ton of friends, both male and female, and a full social schedule, the young doctor seemed content living alone in her upscale condominium, her mother her most frequent visitor.

"Chris?"

She only realized, as she heard her nickname, that she hadn't answered Olivia's question. And that it was too late for a casual shrug accompanied by "Nothing."

"I didn't quite finish dusting Gramps's den," she said. She only had to do one room a day in order for her to keep the big house relatively clean without help.

"Sheila's ready to add you to her client list anytime you say the word," Olivia said, naming her cleaning woman for about the umpteenth time since they'd known each other.

"And why didn't you finish dusting the den?" Olivia called Christine's gaze back to her.

"I have a client who wants me to have his baby for him." There. It was out. Thank God.

"What!" Mouth hanging open, Olivia's eyes were wide, brows raised as she stared at her friend. And then said, "Is he nuts? He thinks your clinic is some kind of freakish baby-making place, a drive-through? And you, personally? Maybe you should think about calling the cops. The guy sounds scary to me."

As a pediatrician specializing in neonatal intensive care, Olivia had seen as many of the emotional family dynamics as Christine had. Probably more.

"No." And suddenly she didn't want to say any more. Jamison wasn't a freak. His request, while bordering on inappropriate, given the circumstances, hadn't been the least bit frightening. Or even, considering those same circumstances, out of place. "His wife died a year ago. They have frozen embryos. She thought I would be a good surrogate."

"You know her?"

Where on earth were their salads? "I met her once. They were Parent Portal clients."

"You want to do this." Olivia had gone still. Was studying her closely.

"I told him no way." She'd told him to get out

of her office. She cringed every time she thought about it. "But that, even though we aren't a surrogacy clinic, I would help him find his surrogate. I've got people I can call. I can act as his proctor without steering the clinic someplace we don't want to go, or putting us at risk."

Still no salad. Her one glass of wine wasn't going to last through dinner if she didn't hurry up and get some food.

People came and went around them. Someone from another table cackled loudly. Pop music played softly in the background. She felt like she could hear Olivia thinking. Hear every breath she took. Because she feared that her friend was seeing more of her than she was ready to have discovered. Deciphered. Analyzed and picked apart and contemplated.

Some things were best left to wilt and fade away. It just took time.

And yet, she'd blabbed.

Holding her friend's gaze, she searched for words that would defuse the firecracker she'd just figuratively lit on the table between them.

"Here you go! Sorry for the wait." Christine didn't recognize the young woman who arrived and placed their salads with speed and ease. The waitress added, "Someone else took your order, and then delivered it to the wrong table so it had to be remade. She's new and I do apologize…"

Christine, putting her napkin in her lap and picking up her fork, was happy to have her rattle on. Anything to distract her from Jamison's request.

"You want to be the surrogate."

Christine had eaten most of her salad. Was taking small sips of her wine to make it last longer. Had thought the conversation was done. At least the part that included Olivia. Or anyone else.

"I want to help him. The man's a genuinely nice guy. He and his wife… I wish you could have seen them together. They'd been best friends since they were eight years old…"

She hadn't needed the emergency room story to see the connection between Emily and Jamison Howe. But that piece of history had been replaying itself in her mind ever since the man had left her office. She kept picturing that little girl who, at eight, had been so in tune that she'd received an otherworldly message. Or even just willing to be open enough to reach out when her soul mate arrived in her sphere. Whether or not she'd known that was what Jamison was to her, clearly she'd felt something. And had been trusting enough to believe in that feeling.

Children generally were trusting.

Until they learned through painful lessons to harden the sensitive walls that encased the human heart.

"It's okay, you know." Olivia's gaze was always

filled with intelligence and usually compassion. But the empathy…

"What's okay?"

"You wanting to have this baby for him."

"I didn't say I wanted to. I said no way."

"I know. And I know you. If you didn't want to do it, you'd have let it go already. You'd go to work in the morning, make your calls, get the ball rolling to proctor his surrogate search, and we wouldn't be having this conversation."

"With a fee from being a surrogate, I could get all of the renovations done on the house, including a new dishwasher and garbage disposal, new kitchen countertops, electric garage doors…without taking any higher salary from the clinic."

"You need to pay yourself more than you do, but you aren't sidetracking me with that discussion now," Olivia said.

Maybe she told the other woman too much. She had lots of friends. She needed to spread her news around more. Some to one. Some to another.

It was just that she trusted Olivia in the same way she'd trusted Gram and Gramps. Like she'd trust a sister…

"He's willing to pay living expenses for the duration of time I'd be involved, including recovery, which is somewhat common in the surrogacy world. That would mean my entire salary for all those months would be freed up."

Maybe she could get her bathroom updated. Have new tiles put up in the shower. The colors of the old were so faded she couldn't even be sure someone would recognize the pattern if they hadn't been looking at it for thirty-plus years.

The wooden floors throughout the house were solid, but could stand to be buffed and resurfaced.

"And in addition to that, he's going to make a contribution to the clinic—not a surrogacy fee, just a donation…"

"You'd be asking a lot of yourself," Olivia said. "Having your body change, the hormones, morning sickness, fatigue, back pain…"

Yeah, and no wine. She gulped at the liquid barely filling the bottom of her glass.

"It'll only be for a matter of months, realistically," she said. "You don't even show the first two or three months. A lot of women don't even know they're pregnant until two or three months. And the fourth month, okay, maybe some morning sickness, but otherwise your pants just fit a little more tightly."

She stopped herself. Chilled and a bit light-headed as she heard, in her mind, where her words had been headed. Olivia knew a lot about her. But not about Ryder. That was her name for her son, not the one the boy had been given by his parents. She had no idea what name was on his birth certificate. First, middle or last.

No one in her current life in Marie Cove knew

about Ryder. Her father knew, but not because he'd been around. Gram and Gramps had had custody of her by then and had agreed not to tell her father. And going five months without seeing her father, to keep him ignorant of her pregnancy, would have been surprisingly, heartbreakingly, easy. He hadn't seemed to notice when that much time had passed in between visits. But his health insurance company had sent a bill for the ultrasound...

Or rather, she'd thought no one in her current life knew about Ryder.

She'd told Emily Howe—with Jamison sitting there beside her.

"I'm not sure if you want kids of your own," Olivia was saying, blissfully not seemingly in tune with quite every thought in Christine's mind. "But have you even thought about what it would be like to have one growing inside you? To feel him moving, a part of you...how would you not fall at least a little bit in love? And then to have to give it up?"

Now there was an easy answer. "I'd be giving him or her to someone who wants only to love and support him, who has the means and the desire to give him a happy and secure life in a world filled with love.

"And besides," she added, blurting words out of the panic that had nearly consumed her seconds before, "I'm not sure I can be a surrogate. All of the clinics require that you've delivered at least one healthy baby. I'd have to check to see if, in private surrogacy, that stipulation still exists."

"I'm not sure it does," Olivia said.

Not an issue for her. She'd basically just lied to her best friend by omission, and it made her feel kind of sick.

"I guess, when you think about it, no one can stop you from having a baby if you want to. And, legally, you can work out any custody or adoption arrangements you want to, as long as the recipient of the child passes adoption inspections, but with the proposed recipient actually the biological parent, then that wouldn't be an issue. You'd just need to make sure he couldn't ever come after you for child support..."

She'd led Olivia to a wrong path, and her friend, sweetheart that she was, was galloping down it.

"The state of California requires that both parties, no matter who they are, have separate surrogacy lawyers," she said, needing to get them both going in another direction.

Olivia finished her wine. Grabbed the bill that had been left before Christine could do so, and the two of them walked out to Christine's car. They'd driven over from the center together.

She asked her friend about a project she was working on at the hospital, something to do with a research study that measured the health benefits of reading to babies, in an effort to get a library set up in the neonatal intensive care unit. Christine had of-fered to help to fundraise for books as soon as the project was approved.

And they talked about a two-day Catalina Island cruise Christine was taking the next weekend. She was going with two of her friends from college, one of whom was going through a divorce.

"You want to tell me why you really want to have this baby?" Olivia asked when she was supposed to be getting out of Christine's car back at the women's center and then into her own just a couple of steps away.

"I told you. The money would help a lot. It's not like I have any family or am in a relationship that would be affected by it. And, as you pointed out, I've never been sure about kids of my own so the emo-tional part wouldn't be such an issue…"

Even if she did want kids of her own, there was nothing to stop her from having another one once the favor was done. Women could give birth mul-tiple times. Her great-grandmother had had four-teen children.

Olivia nodded. Moved to get out. But not before Christine had seen the quickly masked hurt in her eyes. The two of them—they'd bonded over their true desire to live alone. To be single. They were the odd girls out. Those who didn't want to be part of a couple.

And they kept very few secrets from each other.

She had Ryder. And Olivia had whatever it was that kept her single.

"His wife…" she blurted. "Emily. I remember her so distinctly. She got to me, you know?" She'd told her about Ryder. "We went to the same high school. They're from here, but I didn't know them. Still, it felt like she was a friend. And then, to hear that she'd told her husband that if they ever needed a surrogate she thought I'd make a great one…"

Olivia's eyes glistened in the blend of light and shadows.

"Have you ever felt like something stronger than what you can see and prove is at work in a situation?" Christine asked, her voice barely above a whisper. Almost as though she'd taken a lid off the magic potion only to find out that it had no power at all.

"Every day," Olivia said. "I see it in the eyes of the parents who hang on and believe after I've told them that their newborn has little chance of sustaining life. And then, sometimes, in the little ones who prove me wrong."

It was all so confusing. The request. The fact that it was hitting her so strongly. It wasn't the first time she'd had the chance to be a surrogate. There'd been another couple a few years back… They'd both had steady jobs, but an income that wasn't ever going to allow them to be able to pay for one. The fertility testing and drugs had taken all of their savings. Christine had had herself tested, just to make certain she'd be a viable candidate, but before she could offer to help them, the woman's sister had agreed to carry their child...

"You think I'm wrong to be considering this?"

"No. I just hope you really think about it, about how it will feel to carry a baby inside you, to give birth to it and not have it be placed in your arms..."

She didn't have to think about that part. She knew it firsthand. And knew she could deal with it. Which was part of what was pushing her forward.

"That's what I'm doing. Thinking about it. I don't think I'm going to do it. It's like this fantastical episode playing out in my mind, but not real, you know?"

"You're the most practical woman I know," Olivia said, reaching a hand out to her arm, as though knowing Christine needed some connection to ground her back into reality. "If it's on your mind, you're considering it."

Her friend was right. She was considering it. Just wasn't going to do it.

"Whatever you decide, you have my support."

Olivia's parting words were more than a promise. They were like a whisper on the wind beneath Emily's angel's wings, nudging her forward.

Chapter Five

Running forward to make the slam that would win him the match, Jamie came down with his custommade tennis racket and hit the lime-green ball at just the right angle to make his volley impossible to return. The grunt he emitted was for show.

The score—6:4, 7:5, 6:3. He'd just skunked the man who'd been a father to him for more than half his life.

Dropping off their rackets in the lockers they rented at the Marie Cove Country Club, they walked out to the beachside bar that would be filling up as soon as the day's golfers started to wander in. Saturdays were always the busiest, but it was also the only day Emily's father, Judge Tom Sanders, had free that week. He was heading up to wine country on Sunday for a week of boating and fishing with friends, and Jamie needed to speak with him before he left.

They ordered their customary after-a-match beer, toasted to the win and, rather than settling into a seat at the bar, Jamie asked his father-in-law if they could walk.

"You've got something on your mind," the older man said, his graying hair glinting in the sunlight. A couple of inches taller than Jamie, widower Tom was lean and still drew the eyes of the women at the pool and, farther below, in the sand, as, in their tennis shorts, T-shirts and shoes, they headed down a paved walkway at the top of the beach.

"Let me help," Tom continued, his deep baritone as commanding as always. "I've been waiting for the call that would tell me that you've started dating again, and I just want you to know that not only am I prepared to see that happen, I'm hoping for it to happen," he said, holding his beer by his thigh as they walked. He smiled as a woman passed.

Tom watched the woman go, sipped from his beer and faced forward again.

"You know her?"

"She was in my court a couple of months ago. Tough divorce." While Tom had done his stint in criminal court, he'd opted to sit on the civil bench after Emily's accident. It took less of an emotional toll, he'd told Jamie one night when he'd had an un-characteristic amount of alcohol to drink.

"So...back to what I was saying... I want to dispel any sense of guilt you might be feeling..."

"I'm not seeing anyone." And he'd thought what he had to say would be easier. Good news. Instead, he felt like a college kid, again, asking the man if he could marry his daughter.

Confident of Tom's regard, just not certain the older man would understand or condone his request. After all, Emily had always had standing in the community and her parents had a lot of money, while Jamie had been the son of a woman who worked five days a week in an office just to make ends meet.

If it hadn't been for the tennis scholarship Tom had urged him to go after, he'd never have made it into college, much less grad school.

Besides, while he and Em had been close since that long-ago day in the emergency room, they'd taken a long time to get from there to admitting they were more than just friends.

Maybe he was premature in his declaration. He hadn't heard a word from Christine Elliott, but then she'd only had three business days to start putting out feelers on his behalf—or considering taking on the project herself—and it wasn't like he'd be her only professional task. She had a slew of clients. A clinic to run.

A life to live.

There'd been more than a few times he'd shuddered over the memory of what he'd done—making an appointment with a woman he hadn't seen in two years, a woman he'd only met once, to ask her to have his baby.

And yet, while he regretted the manner in which he'd done it, he still knew he couldn't possibly move forward with a family without doing all he could to get Christine to agree to be the one to make it possible for him.

He downed a quarter of his bottle of beer. Let the liquid wash the nervousness away. Tom would be as delighted about the baby as he'd been about Jamie and Emily's engagement. And once Jamie told the judge about his intentions, there'd be no going back.

"I've decided to use the embryos Emily and I froze to start a family." He wasn't looking for permission. Wasn't going to change his mind. And Tom had a right to know that he was going to be a grandfather posthumously. After losing his wife and then his only child, he deserved to know that there was good around the corner.

The man stopped, pulled Jamie off the path and leaned back against a guardrail along the back side of it. "Are you serious?"

Grinning, Jamie nodded. "I've given it a lot of thought, and I know that this is the right thing for me to do."

Tom wasn't smiling. In fact, his frown was one

Jamie had seen the older man use in court a time or two. "I disagree." Tom shook his head. "Strongly."

"But…"

"Have you told your mother about this?"

He was thirty-three years old and a successful, respected educator; Jamie most certainly didn't need his mother's permission for anything. "No. I'm not planning to tell anyone until the fertilization procedure is successful. Except you. I wanted you to know. I thought you had a right to know."

He'd hoped to bring some joy to Tom's life. Had hoped for his support. He was giving Tom the only chance he'd ever have at grandchildren…

"You're a young man, Jamie. You've got your whole life ahead of you. Find a woman. Fall in love. Marry her. And then have a family that belongs to both of you."

"But…"

Shaking his head, Tom interrupted. "I'm telling you, this is a bad idea."

So maybe his reservations of moments ago had been warranted. He'd actually expected Tom to be pleased. Once he got over the possible shock of it.

He'd conceded that Tom might think he wasn't thinking clearly. That he was acting out of grief. Had been prepared to assure him that wasn't the case.

So… Strike two on the "talking with others" part of his plan.

First Christine and now Tom. But he couldn't do

it without them. Not in the way he envisioned, at any rate.

"My son or daughter, he or she is going to need their grandpa." He could be as strong as Tom when warranted.

"Let her go, Jamie."

This was going to be maybe one of the toughest things he'd ever done. He looked Emily's dad straight in the eye and said, "I have let her go, Tom. This isn't about hanging on to the past, or seeking comfort due to loss. This is about getting on with the rest of my life. Those embryos are there. And yes, it's a bit unconventional for me to continue with the plans Emily and I made without her, but it's the life I want. I had my soul mate. I'm thankful for the years we shared. All twenty-five of them. And while I expect I'll eventually start dating again, I'm not looking for another life partner. If Emily had been able to get pregnant when we'd first started trying, we'd already have a four-year-old child. And I'd be raising that child on my own."

Tom was still frowning. Shaking his head. But he no longer looked fierce. At least not to Jamie. "But, son…"

"No, Tom," Jamie said. "My mind is made up about this. I'd hoped you'd be excited. But at the very least, you had a right to know."

"I know how hard it is, Jamie. I've been there. Re-member?" Tom's green eyes grew moist, the wrinkles at the corners of his eyes more pronounced. "When I first lost Daisy..."

Emily's mother had died from hepatitis when he and Emily were in college.

"I know." Jamie gave the man a minute, remembering how awful that year had been, for all of them, but mostly for Emily and her father. For a while there Jamie had wondered if either of them would ever be truly happy again. Daisy had been the hub on their wheel. And then he said, "It's been almost fifteen years and I don't see you dating again."

Sure, Tom looked at women. He even went out to dinner on occasion. But never once had he introduced another woman to Jamie or Emily.

Lips pursed, Tom nodded. "I'm not going to change your mind, am I?"

"No, sir."

"Do you have any idea of the time frame?"

"Not yet."

Tom started back toward the bar, which was still clearly in view, his bottle almost empty. Jamie dropped his half-full one in the trash as they got close. He had a feeling Tom would be drinking one too many and would need a ride home.

Him. He would be his father-in-law's designated driver.

Funny how life had a way of turning on a dime.

Funny how, even before his child was conceived, he was assuming the role of a father.

* * *

Christine lived alone, but she had a busy life. So much so that she didn't even think it fair of her to have a pet. She wasn't home enough. She spent too much time working at the clinic and women's shelter, plus looking after two elderly couples in the area, having her book club, sitting on a committee that was in charge of overseeing community events and maintaining a slew of friends. Marie Cove, her people, were her family, and she was determined to tend to them as she had her grandparents all those years. Just as they'd all been there for her. That's what family did.

And there was racquetball. Because a woman had to tend to herself, too, if she was going to be any good to others.

One lunchtime the following week, after stopping by the Madisons'—neighbors she was checking in on while their daughter was away on a cruise with her husband—she drove by the high school. Parking across the street, she ate the chicken ranch wrap she'd packed that morning and watched as the high school tennis coach oversaw the summer camp that involved those who would try out for the team in the fall.

She'd signed up her freshman year, but hadn't gone. There'd been so much to do at home, and she'd never have been able to make it to team practices and be gone for all the matches, even if she'd made the team...

Maybe if the coach back then had been as good-looking as Dr. Jamie Howe...

As a coach, Jamie was demonstrating a serve, and those legs... They looked like pure muscle. Lean and strong as iron.

And were absolutely none of her business.

She'd reread his file, in preparation for helping him find a surrogate that would be a good match after she told him no. She was just waiting for him to call and ask her what she'd decided.

She couldn't hear what he was saying out on the court, but the way the kids gathered around him, watched him as he spoke, kept close, approached him, performed for him, she couldn't help thinking he'd make one heck of a good dad.

If he was as patient at home as he appeared to be on the court. And as well-liked...

A person who looked like she might be one of the players' moms approached the court, and Jamie went to speak to her. Her wrap finished, Christine put her car in gear and drove straight back to her office, wiping any thoughts of those male legs out of her psyche.

By the second week since Jamison Howe's visit, she wasn't thinking about the man's legs at all. It had been ten days without a word from him. Seven grueling games of one-person racquetball.

She hadn't figured him for someone who would not call. Had been on edge that whole first week after he'd been to see her, thinking he'd be contacting her at any moment. Waiting for the call. The email. The text. Not because she couldn't get the man out of her system, but because his request continued to linger there. She knew she was going to tell him no, and had to fight with herself, trying not to picture what it would be like if she said yes.

She'd pictured it anyway. The hardships involved with being pregnant. The joy she'd be bringing him. The honor he'd given her—the honor *Emily* had given her. The money that would help her get the house she'd inherited back in pristine condition.

And give added security to the clinic as well.

The hardships would be only temporary.

She thought about them, though, as she cruised to Catalina Island and back with her friends, not that she told either them about the client she'd had or his unusual request. None of them talked about work at all. They spent the two days having fruity drinks by the pool, playing trivia games against other ship passengers, eating decadently and shopping. The other two laughed over stupid things they'd done in college, mostly having to do with guys, and told Christine she'd been the smart one all along to avoid all that heartache.

By the time she returned on Sunday, two days short of two weeks since Jamie had been to her office, she'd quit waiting for the phone to ring. Or for the athletic math professor to show up at her office door. And while she had to admit to being a bit let down—at least to herself—she also knew that if his interest had been that short-lived, she'd been saved making a huge mistake in even considering having a child for him. Or finding another woman to do so.

A baby was a lifetime commitment.

He must have had a change of heart. Maybe he'd realized that it would better to move on and wait to have a family in a traditional way, with a woman who'd be there to help him raise any children they had.

Still, it would have been nice if he'd at least called to let her know. For all he knew, she could have been making calls, finding contacts, maybe even finding surrogates for him to interview. She'd said she'd proctor for him and he hadn't called to tell her not to do so.

That's when it began to niggle at her that something could have happened to him. In the week since she'd spent a lunch hour playing voyeur outside the high school. And peevishness started to stab at her a bit, too.

So thinking, that last Friday in May, seventeen days after they'd met, she called him, intending to inquire as to any further services he might need from The Parent Portal so that, finding none, she could get his file off her desk.

It was time to declutter.

"Christine." He picked up before the first ring

had finished. "I was beginning to think you weren't going to call."

What? They hadn't left it that she'd call him.

They'd just…left it.

With her saying she'd agree to his request to think about his original request. Sort of. And with her possibly checking on some things for him pursuant to surrogacy, yes, but…

Wouldn't you then expect he'd check back in, to see…?

"I was waiting for you to call," she told him. "After we both had time to think. I did speak with my attorney regarding The Parent Portal assisting you with your surrogate search, and made some calls, but when I didn't hear from you again…"

Patients made appointments with medical facilities. That's how it worked. She had a personal service to offer. He had to avail himself of it. And had the right to change his mind and not do so. It wasn't up to her to hound him about it.

Had it been a matter of life and death, then certainly, a clinic or doctor might call a patient as a gentle, or not so gentle, reminder, but in her business…

Infertility was a tough thing. It wasn't her place to push. Clinics had clients who came to them, who seemed to want their services, and then they never heard from them again. It was in the nature of their business.

"I was actually just doing a follow-up, assuming, since I hadn't heard from you that I could close your file…" The emotion storming through her didn't quite give truth to those words.

"No! Please. Nothing has changed, not as far as I'm concerned. Should I make another appointment for us to speak?"

No! Her thoughts echoed his word. "Yes, that would be best," she told him. "I can put you through to reception. Hold on…"

Without giving him a chance to say anything further, she clicked a button on the phone, and another, turned the call over and hung up.

Trying not to notice how much her hand was shaking.

Or to admit that her life was about to take a detour she hadn't expected.

Chapter Six

The first appointment he could get was Tuesday at one—a full three weeks since the last time he'd been to Christine Elliott's office. He'd have liked to have changed from the clothes he'd worn to tennis camp that morning, as planned, but had been waylaid by a student who'd wanted to speak with him. Axel Barrymore, a fatherless kid, was getting pressure from his mother to concentrate on basketball because of scholarship opportunities. This discussion was not something from which Jamie could walk away. He'd ended up speaking with both Axel and his mother, told them that Axel was better at tennis than he'd ever been, a natural, but that the boy needed to choose the sport he loved the most. He'd offered to make himself available in the future, anytime either of them needed anything. And hoped he'd helped.

He was thirty seconds from being late to his own appointment.

"I'm coming straight from tennis camp," he admitted, as he noticed the way the health administrator was looking at his bare legs.

"No, you're fine," Christine said, arranging various papers in front of her—a few side by side, a few in stacks.

To do with him? Surrogate possibilities?

He tried to meet her gaze, to assess her state of mind, but she was too busy to look up. And then her phone rang and she answered it.

Figuring he knew the drill, he sat in the chair he'd occupied twice in the past. Knowing that whatever happened, he was taking the next step forward to having his family. The rush that swept through him took him a bit by surprise.

He wasn't prone to emotional outbursts. Or *in*bursts, as the case might be. Even in grief he hadn't been overwrought. He'd been able to rationalize. To cry alone. And then do what had to be done.

Still on the phone, Christine's conversation was mostly one-sided. She had said little except for an occasional "uh-huh," "yes" and "I'm listening."

He noticed his finger tapping on his knee and stilled. Tried not to put too much emphasis on the fact that, depending on what information was hiding in those papers, he could be closer than he'd realized to becoming a father.

And wouldn't dwell on the disappointment he'd feel if the surrogate were someone other than Christine. Surely Emily would understand that he'd tried...

She wouldn't understand. That wasn't her way. When Emily knew something, she stuck to her guns. Even if she was wrong. Like the house. It was on the market—finally. And he was due to take at least a ten-thousand-dollar hit because of it.

He was tapping again. Watching his thumb and finger for a moment, then stilled them again. Picked at a thread on the hem of his shorts.

He heard the phone drop in the cradle.

"Sorry about that," Christine said, her gaze landing on him with the force of a blow. Those big brown eyes, so filled with...something he couldn't define.

Which put him on edge.

More on edge.

"I was just speaking with my doctor," she said then, standing and heading to the other side of her office—behind him—where he knew a conversation area with a couch and chairs sat. He heard a refrigerator door open, turned to see a small one set into the cupboards set along the far wall.

"Would you like some water?" she asked. "Or juice? I have pineapple, peach and cranberry..."

He preferred orange, hated pineapple, but said, "Peach, please."

He didn't want any juice, really.

Had she just said she'd been on the phone with her doctor? He knew she had. But...

"I've decided to grant your request to be the surrogate for your embryo," she said, sounding like a high school principal or something as she walked slowly back toward her desk, stopping to place a cold bottle of capped juice on the corner of the desk closest to him.

She didn't hand it to him. Why did he notice? Or care?

"That is, if you still would like to consider me as a prospect," she added, watching him as she retook her seat behind the desk. "You'd said that you hadn't changed your mind when we spoke at the end of last week."

"I haven't!" He sat up. Stood up. Reached for the juice. Sat back down. "Did you just say yes?" he asked inanely. He knew there was absolutely nothing wrong with his hearing.

It was the rest of his brain that concerned him. The scattered messages it was sending... Spiked with huge hits of adrenaline...

"I did." Christine wasn't smiling. She didn't look angry, either. Just professional.

Right. Which was what he should be doing. Acting like the professional he was.

"I'm sorry," he said, taking a sip of juice and holding the bottle on the arm of the chair. "I just...you took me by surprise." The grin that evolved out of the waywardness of his mouth almost split his lips. "This is great!" he said. Smiling some more. Nodding. And then, "Seriously, I... Wow. Thank you."

There, finally, something appropriate to the moment.

And then, as though that expression of gratitude righted his mind, a mental list appeared in his thought process.

"So...we'll need to take care of the legalities..."

She handed him one of the piles of papers. "My portion is all here for your lawyer to look over," she said. "I've already had my stipulations drawn up. I'm sure you'll have your own, and when you get back to me, I'll have a meeting with my attorney and hopefully we'll end up with a final document with which we can both be satisfied."

He didn't give a damn if she wanted to name the child. He'd be satisfied. Hopefully appearing a whole lot more calm on the outside than he felt on the inside, he reached for the papers.

Holy hell. He and Emily were going to have their baby! With Christine, just like Emily had envisioned.

His wife hadn't been planning to die. Or even been aware that she might. He didn't think that for a second. But, in her way, when she'd told him that if they had to use a surrogate she thought it should be Christine, she'd still planned their future. Just like that day in the emergency room when she'd called him over and asked him to be her friend. Those words—"see ya" instead of goodbye.

He wanted to pick Emily up and swing her around and around like he had on the dance floor at their wedding reception. To sweep her right up off her feet. To hug her tight.

Glanced to his right. Saw the empty chair sitting next to him.

And welled up with tears.

If Christine hadn't looked up from her papers— she wouldn't have noticed the tears glistening in Jamison Howe's eyes for the second he took to blink.

And then they were gone and he was watching her.

"Anything else?" he asked, not quite smiling, but looking pleased. He held up the papers she'd pushed toward him with one hand, the bottle of juice in the other, and her heart leaped. The man was too endearing to go to waste. He had to find another woman to love. To have her children.

"I've already had the medical exams and tests necessary," she said. "That was my doctor's office on the phone, giving me the final report."

"Your doctor's office isn't here?" An innocuous question. She hadn't realized how badly she'd needed it. Something to get her focus back where it belonged.

"I do see one of our doctors, but I go to her office."

"So you're good to go?"

"As soon as I ovulate." Okay, that was awkward. She'd never talked to a guy about her cycle before. Not even Nathan, Ryder's father. Two loves she didn't allow herself to think about...

Because they were both gone from her life forever. One by his choice, the other by hers.

"I stipulate in there that I want to use my own fertility specialist—the same one who worked with you and Emily so I'm assuming that won't be a problem—and my own ob-gyn for the delivery. You can speak to either of them about the fertilization process if you'd like."

He shook his head. "I'd just as soon hear it from you. That is, if you don't mind and it's appropriate."

Yeah. Right. That. She sighed. "This whole thing is a little...off the normal course..." she told him. "But not at all illegal," she quickly asserted. "As long as we both have separate lawyers who are well versed in surrogacy law, and sign an agreed upon contract, we're fine. I'll be acting as an individual, not in any official capacity with The Parent Portal," she added, getting back on track again. "It was decided that that was best, easiest and the least risk to the clinic. It's all in there." She pointed to the unsigned contract she'd handed him. "I'm choosing to use our fertility specialist and one of our ob-gyns, but as a private client, with private billing. So you'll need to do the same. You'll need to pay the doctors directly, not through the clinic."

Which meant costs could likely be a little higher. Her doctors gave The Parent Portal a preferred rate— as they did all of the fertility clinics they worked with.

"It's generally recommended that surrogacy participants go through an agency for the entire process, but I'm only going to be able to do this for you if we have a private arrangement."

Because she'd made that choice. She wasn't going to do anything that in any way impacted the clinic. Or even had a chance of doing so.

He was nodding. Seemingly unfazed. And she didn't know if she was relieved or not. She was really offering to do this. But did she hope that he'd change his mind? Balk at the stipulations? These were all nonnegotiable, as he'd see when he actually looked at the contract, which started on the page beneath the preface letter from her lawyer she'd seen him looking at.

"You'll notice an escrow agreement in there, as well as your right to prove that I've undergone both medical and emotional screening and have passed both."

There'd been no point in spending time thinking about whether or not she could grant the Howes' request without knowing that she had the ability to do so.

"And there are insurance stipulations as well."
He'd need to purchase a special surrogacy plan on
her behalf, with all premiums paid up front so that if
anything happened to him, or if he was in breach of
contract, her and the baby's health would still be covered. If his own health insurance didn't offer a plan,
there were plenty in the state of California that did.

She'd been taking care of her "family" for too
long to put any of them—her home, the clinic, its
employees and clients—at risk.

He still hadn't done more than glance at the cover
page of the document. "So what's the process from
here? Once I have my attorney look this over and it's
signed," he said, holding up the contract.

Glancing down, she took in the other small piles
in front of her, deciding which to choose next. Her
face warm, she was embarrassed. Feeling his pres-
ence like she'd never felt a client—or anyone else—
in her life. As though he was touching her from
across the desk. As though she wanted him to.

It was because she was planning to have his baby.
She knew that. They had, and would continue to
have, purely a business arrangement between the two
of them. She knew that, too. What they were doing
was completely accepted and professional. But when
it involved your most intimate parts...

She chose the calendars first—a page for each
month she'd be under his employ. "This is the ten-
tative schedule I've worked out," she said. "This is

based on all of the information I've gathered and on when giving birth would fit best in my schedule." The dates were all in the contract, too. "This is all assuming that, biologically, everything happens as expected." The contract held a caveat that the dates could change, without consent needed, if things didn't work out the first time around.

He looked at every single page. She hadn't intended him to read the specifics about the various pregnancy-related appointments she'd be having during her prenatal care. Not right then, at any rate.

The last pages were a repeat of July and August, with implantation dates again, instead of ob-gyn appointments.

"What's this?" he asked, holding up those last two pages.

"Those start the original cycle over, a month and two later, in case it takes more than one implantation to result in pregnancy." The contract gave him three tries with her body before they'd reassess her viability.

He went back to the first page. And she slid the last pile of papers across her desk. "This is all reading material I've gathered about the procedure. There's a sheet in the back that gives a list of credible surrogacy clinics if you decide you'd rather go that route. Or even just call and talk to someone before you take this on. They have all kinds of resources available to you..."

He was already shaking his head. "I've done my homework," he said, meeting her gaze openly. And then he smiled. "I just can't believe you said yes," he said. And then continued, "Except that in my mind, I knew you would. I also knew that thought made no sense."

Her life had to make sense. Always. And this did, helping him. She'd held a staff meeting, let everyone know what she was contemplating and why. Every single one of them had offered their support and told her how much they admired her for what she was doing.

Of course, she was their employer, but the doctors who worked with her certainly didn't need her as much as she needed them.

"I'm assuming we'll be doing this on your regular cycle then, instead of having you on fertility drugs that will regulate you to a specific date, since the embryos aren't going to be freshly prepared." He'd ignored the contract, but this he was reading.

"That's right," she said. Which was why his original question about timeline had had her blurting out about her ovulation. "Five days after mid-cycle is best as it generally takes a naturally forming embryo that long to travel through the fallopian tube."

Talking about their reproductive parts was routine at The Parent Portal. Discussing them with Jamison Howe made her a little uncomfortable. Embarrassed.

And kind of like she was getting a little bit naked in front of him.

Speaking of which…

"I'm assuming you'll want to be present for medical visits, but I reserve the right to have my privacy protected," she said.

The child she'd be growing was his. Not hers. He had a right to be there for each step of its growth.

"You have a choice to make," she told him, gesturing with a nod toward the calendars he'd put on the edge of the desk. "We can do a mock injection to make sure we have timing right with my cycle if you'd like, before using any of the embryos. They implant more than one each time, and since you've got a limited number and no guarantee that it will take, my doctor made the offer… They can follow a non-embryonic injection to see if my uterus is ready to accept implantation so many days after I ovulate…"

Oftentimes the mock trial was done when the embryo was being freshly prepared from a mother's egg, because the surrogate had to take fertility drugs to put her cycle in line with the mother's. But, in this case, because the embryos were so critically limited, her doctor had suggested Jamison might want to do that. Christine was an expert on fertility, as much as she could be without a medical degree, but she'd learned some things over the past couple of weeks.

He shook his head. "No, I'm fine with going ahead," he said. "I don't want to put you through anything more invasive than necessary. And from the reading I did, the mock trial is generally done when the embryos are being freshly prepared…"

She was impressed. And oddly comforted. The man wasn't just acting on a whim. He knew his stuff.

He picked up the calendar again. "So it looks like June 7 is our day?"

Ten days away.

"Assuming we come to a contractual agreement."

He nodded. Stood. Held out his hand.

So she shook it. As she'd done with many, many clients over the years. Probably including him and his wife.

So why, as he thanked her again, holding her gaze, seemingly letting her read into his depths, did she suddenly feel as though, with that simple, professional touch of the hand, she'd just agreed to a crazy kind of love?

Chapter Seven

Jamie had his attorney add one clause to the contract in the coming days, allowing Christine the right to have contact with the child. And also, if at any time the resultant child wanted contact, Jamie could call her and let her know, with the decision to meet up to her.

There'd be a bond there.

And Christine's life work was about the human element involved in fertility science.

His son or daughter was going to know that his or her biological mother had passed away a year before conception. That child might want to know Christine. Conceivably, he or she might feel some gratitude. Hopefully. If Jamie did his job right.

Everything else about the contract was solid. Appropriate. Even the living expense amount—exactly to the penny of the average projected cost in the state of California, according to Jamie's lawyer.

He'd have signed it even if it had been hugely one-sided. Two days after the meeting, he stayed on the court for a couple of hours after tennis camp, hitting balls with anyone who wanted to play with him, while he waited for the call from his attorney telling him that she'd signed the final contract that had been hand delivered to her that morning.

He'd offered, at the beginning of camp, to make himself available to any of the attendees who wanted some one-on-one time with him. He hadn't expected the twelve-student lineup, but allotted each of them fifteen minutes after which they could go to the end of the line and wait for a second session.

The May air was balmy. Low 70s. The court protected from direct sun by the school's amphitheater behind which they sat.

He gave the private sessions a few times every year during camp. Usually setting a stopping point before he began, but that day he didn't. That day he needed the session more than his students did. That day they were helping him.

And when the call came, at just after three, telling him the deal was signed and legally recorded, he shared the news with the seven students left on the court with him. And took them all out for ice cream to celebrate.

He was back in the father game.

And he was going to be a good one.

She was good at her job. Able to care deeply, to empathize, sympathize, bleed compassion and keep a personal distance at the same time. To Christine, doing so was a no-brainer. A happy life meant taking care of who and what you loved.

Others told her she had a gift.

Whatever. She didn't see it that way.

She was just appreciative of her ability to remain personally impassive that first Friday morning in June as she was undressing in the small, a little too cold procedure room in the offices of her fertility doctor's private practice.

She didn't allow herself to dwell on the man sitting outside reception, waiting for his child to be conceived. Other than to remember that she was working for him.

As she'd talked to Olivia the night before, over her last glass of wine for the next nine months, she'd told her friend that she kind of saw what she was doing as the same kind of thing as a soldier going to war. Soldiers gave their lives, their bodies, to their country for the time they spent in their attempts to provide citizens with the freedom they deserved. She was signing on for nine months of service to provide a family with a deserving citizen. She was helping one man win the fight against infertility and a tragedy that had taken away his family.

Her whole life's work was about helping to create families. The Parent Portal was the home that housed all of the people who were "family" to her. And as the doctor and a nurse came in, explained the process one more time, asked her if she was ready, Christine positioned herself as instructed, smiled and nodded.

It was just another task for work.

She'd driven herself to the doctor's office. Jamie had offered to pick her up, but she'd said she was going into work first, taking care of a few things, making certain a few others were ready to go and then she'd meet him at the fertility specialist's office. He'd had the appointment prior to Christine's, to meet with the doctor, hear about the procedure, along with the same list of instructions Christine would be receiving. He'd known that she'd be required to wait awhile after the procedure before she could leave, had offered to go in and sit with her, but she'd opted to work.

He sat in a chair by the window of the reception area and watched videos on his phone. Birthing videos. Pregnancy videos. Diaper changing videos. And a couple of monster truck competitions.

And every time he heard the door open to the inner rooms, he looked up. When he was the last person in the waiting room, he slid his phone into the back pocket of his black dress shorts and paced a bit.

Tom had called the night before, asking if he wanted a boy or a girl. The judge had tried one more time to talk Jamie into waiting to have a family with a woman he could fall in love with and marry, have children with, but Jamie had heard a note of anticipation in the older man's voice that had been missing for a long time.

Maybe since Daisy had died.

This baby was going to be well loved. Boy or girl. Jamie honestly didn't care which. Whether he had a little Emily or a little him, he was good. Tom didn't have a preference, either. But he had a plethora of plans that they could all do together as a family, from Disneyland to touring the country's capital.

When the door finally opened, after all that waiting, he wasn't at all prepared to see Christine. Or, more accurately, prepared for how beautiful she looked to him. Her short hair, all thick and curling in different directions at the end, like she'd just been blown away by great sex. Those brown eyes that showed surprise when they landed on him.

"I didn't think you'd still be here."

"Of course I'm here," he said. "The contract stipulates that I be an active participant from the very beginning. The baby needs to hear my voice so I'm recognized at birth."

"Yes, but…we don't even know if I'm pregnant

yet." She came closer. Looked kind of tired. Which was expected. She'd just spent a good bit of time lying down.

"You have to take it easy for the next couple of days. Rest," he said. Which was one of the reasons she'd chosen Friday rather than Thursday or Saturday for the implantation. So she could take the weekend to lie low.

"I know," she told him, a tad peevishly.

He was being a pain in the ass already. He got it. Walked with her to the door and blinked as the bright sun hit him in the face. If she didn't like him discussing the instructions with her, she really wasn't going to like what he had in mind next.

"I'm planning to make dinner for you tonight," he told her as they approached their separate vehicles. "And to clean the dishes and whatever other chores you might need doing."

With her hand on her car door—a somewhat older burnt orange small SUV—she turned to him. "Dr. Howe. Seriously..."

"It's in the contract," he said. She'd had it drawn up to her specification. He'd read it thoroughly. "You've given me the right to be a part of everything. This rest period between implantation and pregnancy is critical."

"And you only have a limited number of embryos, two of which were used today," she said, nodding. "Plus you're paying for my services and you're right,

I did give you the right to as much access as you wanted. I just didn't envision…well, we'll figure it out as we go. Remember, the success rate is estimated at only around sixty percent, so I might not even be pregnant yet. But…for now, okay, fine. This is all brand-new and we're finding our way. But I already have dinner in the refrigerator. I made up a chicken enchilada casserole last night. You can heat it up and clean up afterward. You stay downstairs and you leave when I've had enough company and need some privacy. That's in the contract, too. *My* privacy."

Grinning, Jamie nodded.

He'd expected to have to fight a lot harder to get in her front door.

And was looking forward to the evening ahead more than he'd looked forward to anything in a very long time.

It was all very practical. The plans. The rationales. The contract. The process.

She'd managed to compartmentalize the actual procedure as little different from an ordinary vaginal exam. In her world, implantation was all part of their day's work.

One key element was unaccounted for, however. What in the hell was she supposed to do with an incredibly sexy and far too endearing man in her home when he wasn't there for anything to do with *her*? It wasn't like she could suddenly install some kind of X-ray system on her stomach that would allow him to watch over the seed inside her while leaving the rest of her life alone.

And what was with all of the sudden spirals going on "down there"? Did having an embryo implanted inside you suddenly make you horny?

She'd expected cramping. Knew hormones could ratchet up the sex drive. But implantation? She'd never heard of that.

He had dinner in the oven. Was opening cupboards in her kitchen, judging by the sounds. While she lay on the couch, tablet in hand, pretending to work.

She'd just had a new life planted inside her. It was all a little nerve-racking.

"Do you eat at the dining room table or the kitchen?" He came through a small hallway from the kitchen, wiping his hands on the hand towel she'd had hanging from the oven door handle.

"I usually sit at the kitchen counter bar." There were two stools. The kitchen table was for when she had guests over. The dining room for special occasions…

He wasn't a guest.

Thank goodness.

The guy just had to breathe and she was aware of him there. In her home. Filling her space. Those tight, firm legs. The backside that followed suit to form a shape made for A-list actors. She stared at it as he left the room.

It had been a while since she'd had sex. A year or two. Clearly too long.

It was a little late now to do something about that. She couldn't very well go have sex while she was carrying another man's baby.

If the procedure was successful, she wouldn't be having sex for another nine months. Just didn't seem right to have another man's body part up there with a baby trying to grow. Didn't seem the least bit sexy to her. That would make it two or three years going without.

She hadn't thought this through well enough.

Why hadn't Olivia reminded her about this?

Olivia. She'd promised her friend she'd text her when she got home. So thinking, she pulled out her phone and let Olivia, who was in San Diego attending a conference, know that all had gone well. That she was home and resting as planned.

She didn't mention that she wasn't heating her dinner herself. Just like she didn't mention most of the business meetings she had throughout her days. It wasn't like she and Olivia told each other everything.

Christine wasn't a "tell someone everything" person. Not since her mother had died.

Besides, every moment in every day came filled with new things to explore and talk about. No need to dredge up the moment that just passed…

Or ones that passed long ago. So it was a bit discomfiting to her, half an hour later, to find herself sitting side by side with Jamison Howe at her countertop bar, and finding nothing to talk about. The awkward silence was choking her as, everywhere she looked, every thought that came to mind, was filled with nonbusiness conversation.

You could only mention so many times that you hoped and prayed the procedure took. Or that it would be a hard two weeks, waiting for a definitive answer. She could take a test in a couple of days. And since her hormone levels would be in a state of flux, an early test could be wrong, either way.

They'd mentioned the fact that they had enough embryos for a couple of more tries, at least five times. Or her brain had. She wasn't certain she'd said all the words aloud.

Jamie, as he kept insisting she call him, didn't seem to mind the silence. Maybe he was one of those quiet, silent guys.

Which, considering she didn't usually go for that type, preferring a guy to step right up and say his piece, boded well for her inappropriate sexual attraction to him. And not at all well for the months ahead. She could handle no drinking, carrying around extra weight, throwing up... But months on end with no conversation...?

"My Gram and Gramps used to sit here every single day for lunch." She blurted out the words like an exploding pressure cooker. "Right here, on these two bar stools, him on the stool where you're sitting and her, here." There. Something got out.

Hopefully the most innocuous of the thoughts she'd been having and holding back.

"This was their house?"

She nodded. Ate with her normal healthy appetite. The enchiladas were especially good this time around. "My mom grew up here," she said. "And so did I. In case you haven't noticed, the place is huge. By the time my mom and dad married, the house was already getting to be too much for my gram and gramps to maintain, so the four of them decided to live together. Mom would one day inherit the house, and it wasn't like she and Dad would be able to afford anything as nice with the way property values had risen here."

He helped himself to another enchilada. She felt kind of good about that. Mostly she was the only one who usually knew whether the dinner she'd made had been a success or not.

"I tried not to be too nosy, but I got a look at the den," he said then. Sitting next to each other, they were facing the kitchen, not each other, and she found that it made conversation with him easier. She just had to be certain that, with their stools as close as they needed to be to fit, she didn't turn and knock her knees into his thigh.

That would not be good.

"All those books…and the woodworking of the shelves, even the desk. It was like stepping back in time to an elegant drawing room…"

"The floors need to be redone," she said, almost light-headed with relief that they'd found something to talk about. "And the rug is threadbare." It was wool, though, and she hadn't been able to afford another like it in that size; settling for synthetic had seemed disrespectful to her parents and grands.

"I'm actually using the money I'm making from you to finish the updates I need to make on the house," she told him, envisioning hours of house renovation conversation. She had lots and lots to say on that topic. Research she'd done. Choices she'd already made and some she had yet to make.

People she'd interview to do the work. Some she'd chosen, some she had yet to choose.

"I'm assuming your grandparents must have passed, since you speak of them in past tense and… they aren't here," he said, interrupting her perusal of her house repertoire right when she'd been debating starting with floor refinishers or the roofers who'd just completed the first portion of the work that needed to be done. All with an eye to the baby's safety, of course.

"They died, one right after the other, when I was in college."

"I'm sorry." Her peripheral vision told her he'd glanced her way. She glanced back before she could stop herself. Read more in his gaze than she generally shared with business associates. Clients.

Or any employer she'd ever had.

Alarm bells rang through her entire system—so loud it was a wonder he couldn't hear them. They had nine months ahead of them, hopefully, at the very least.

No way could she afford to feel things for this man. *Any* things.

Not even the compassion she freely poured over her clients.

He'd already used up his allotted amount.

Chapter Eight

So the man understood grief. Considering their circumstances, that was a given. Didn't mean they had to share a moment over it.

Turning back to her food, Christine attacked the next bite with a gusto she didn't feel. Not for the chicken. "It wasn't unexpected," she said, finding her distance again. "They'd both been failing for a while."

And her turning up pregnant her senior year of high school hadn't helped matters. She'd caused them so much worry...

Not "Jamie Howe on the premises" thoughts. "I'm sure they're both sighing in relief as they look down and see the new roof," she said, managing a real

chuckle, as she made her first house renovation conversation choice.

"What about your parents? Are they still local?"

He didn't know her. He knew about Ryder, but
he didn't know her. As big and wide as her world
in Marie Cove was, she still lived a somewhat insu-
lar life. Around people who knew about her mom,
at least.

"My mom died when I was ten," she told him.
Clinic history. All of her employees knew. Some of
her clients did. No reason her temporary employer
shouldn't.

Or were they business partners? Their contract
put her mostly in the boss position…

"Dad was working eighty hours a week in LA and
he and my grandparents thought it in my best interest to keep me with them. Eventually he gave them
custody of me." After he remarried.

"I didn't get along with his new wife. Probably
my fault as much as hers. I wasn't open to replacing
my mother. Or having another one."

"Do you ever see them?"

"Once or twice a year. But we talk at least once
a month." She loved her dad. And Tyler, too. Even
had developed some fond feelings for her stepmom,
who'd been a surprising source of support to her
when she'd been pregnant the first time, and again
when Gram had died.

But a girl didn't forget how easily she'd been given

up. Or how easily months could pass without being missed. She knew that love didn't always mean having someone who shared your daily life. Or cared about knowing your daily ups and downs.

"How about you?" He'd almost finished his dinner. As had she. Another awkward moment or two and she'd be escaping. She hoped his response came in time, though. She was kind of curious.

"My mom remarried when I was fourteen. They stayed here in Marie Cove until I graduated, but moved to his hometown in Oregon when I left for college."

"Do you ever see them?" She purposely repeated his question.

"Once or twice a year," he said. "But we talk at least once a month."

He was grinning. She grinned back.

And, on that note, excused herself.

He couldn't get her out of his mind. Being on break at the university didn't help. No papers to grade or club meetings to attend. He'd finished putting together his syllabi for the upcoming semester, too. School hadn't yet started.

A guy could only run so much. Tennis camp was done. He'd picked his team the week before the implantation. Axel, the student whose mother had wanted him to concentrate on basketball, was on it. The team was running regular workouts and practice matches. They were done by eleven, Saturday morning.

Heading to the country club, he'd just pulled into the parking lot when he got a text from Tom. His father-in-law wasn't going to make their tennis date. The daughter of a friend of his had just been arrested. Tom wanted to see what he could do to help.

He was there. He could at least get some lunch. The club's chef had a special sauce he put in his turkey wraps…

Phone still in hand, he pushed the newest icon on his speed dial app.

Christine answered on the first ring with: "I'm fine." And followed it with: "And I don't need a thing."

He pictured her on the couch as he'd left her the night before, her tablet and phone at hand as, propped up by pillows, she worked. She was the clinic's chief fundraiser and was setting up appointments with the boards of various corporations who supported The Parent Portal. She'd told him that the night before when, after dishes, he'd tried to hang around.

After her response, he'd been dismissed. Politely. Kindly. And he'd quickly said good-night, feeling as though he'd left a vital part of himself behind. His and Emily's baby could be in that house.

"Have you had lunch?"

"No, but I've got plenty of food here, Jamie. I

shopped before the procedure. I really am a big girl and perfectly capable of taking care of myself."

"I'm being a pain in the ass."

"No, you're a man who wants to be a part of his baby's life from day one. Assuming the implantation even took. I do understand. I just don't see any sense in us sitting around staring at each other."

"I was going to offer to bring you the best turkey wrap you've ever had. I can drop it and go," he offered, trying to sweeten the deal.

"The best turkey wrap I've ever had is at the country club," she said. "If you can beat that, you're on."

"How about if I tie it? That's where I am."

"I didn't picture you for a golfing guy."

"I'm not. Takes too long. I was here to play tennis, but my match got canceled." He had a life. A good, full one. Why it was suddenly important to him that she knew that, he wasn't sure. Didn't care to ponder the situation.

She'd already accepted implantation of his child. He didn't have to impress her.

"Oh."

"Tom Sanders, my father-in-law, and I play most Saturdays." He was suddenly moved to put his family—his baby's family, too—into the picture.

"Tom Sanders is your father-in-law? Judge Tom Sanders?"

"Yes." A heat wave of worry passed through him. As though he'd done something wrong. Talking to

the woman carrying his child about his wife's father... "You know him?"

There was no reason for awkwardness. The child
he'd had implanted in Christine was Emily's as much
as it was his. He was in no way being unfaithful to
his wife.

It wasn't wrong to like the woman who'd be bringing their child to life. To admire her.

What kind of fool would choose someone he
didn't like, trust a woman he didn't admire, to keep
his baby safe?

"I met him once," Christine was saying. "At a
fundraiser, actually. A dinner put on by the Wentworth Corporation."

Lionel Wentworth, a local financier, was a friend
and golfing buddy of Tom's. Jamie had seen him
once or twice, in passing, at the club.

"You know the Wentworths?"

"Not really. I know Margot Simmons, an employee of theirs. She's in charge of their charitable
donations. I sought her out several years ago, asking for a donation, and she's graciously included us
on her recipient list every year since."

A thread tying them all together.

Relaxing back in the seat of his dark blue SUV, he
watched a couple get out of their luxury sedan and
head into the restaurant. He was no longer part of a
couple. But he was going to need a car seat.

"I'm house hunting this afternoon, but I'd be

happy to drop a wrap off to you," he said. More eager than ever to see her. A decent guy felt gratitude toward those helping him.

"I'd eat it, if you did," she said.

Not quite a request—Christine was far too independent for that—but Jamie was already out of his vehicle, phone still to his ear, heading in to place their order. He'd eat his on the way—saved him from sitting alone in the restaurant, noticing all the couples enjoying their Saturday relaxation time together.

He wasn't ready for that yet.

He'd get there at some point... With another woman.

"You like pickles?"

"And onions and tomatoes."

As did he. Easy order.

"I'll be there shortly..."

He rang off, happier than he'd been in a long time. He was on his way to being a father.

Alive. With a future stretching before him.

He'd definitely made the right decision.

On Sunday Christine watched her phone. Carried it with her from room to room as she dusted the rooms she'd missed for two days. She took it easy. Did light dusting where necessary, using a wand instead of climbing up to get the scrolls at the top of the grandfather clock in the dining room.

When she found herself carrying her phone with

her to the bathroom, she had to acknowledge that she was waiting for Jamie to call. The wrap he'd dropped off the day before had been enough for two meals. She'd thoroughly enjoyed it. Took a moment to wonder what he might offer to bring over for dinner.

And realized that she was enjoying being spoiled a little bit.

Not good.

Yes, she had to give him access to the intimacies involved in her process of giving birth. Not physical intimacies, of course, but the information involving them. And physical access...

She could even enjoy the process, like she enjoyed her work in general. And certain aspects of it more.

But there had to be a balance. Clear boundaries.

Allowing him to tend to her some was fine. Looking forward to that attentiveness crossed boundaries.

Which was why, when he called a little after noon, and her lower belly jumped with approval just at the sight of his name on her screen, she accepted his offer to bring over a healthy portion of a mixed green salad with mangoes and grilled chicken, but didn't invite him in to eat with her.

And as soon as she'd finished her solitary meal, she got in her car and headed over to the women's center. It wasn't her night to be there, but she knew what to do when she started to struggle with anything. Go help someone.

That night she watched a couple of toddlers, sitting on the padded floor of the playroom and interacting with them, distracting them, while their bruised mother sat a couple of doors down. She was talking to the police and accepting arrangements for overnight housing for her and her children.

Christine was there until after ten and half fell in love. And when the embattled little family waited to hear where a room was available, she thought about offering to take them home with her.

She couldn't, of course. She wasn't licensed nor was her home equipped to serve as a safe house. But it felt good to care.

It always did.

On Monday, Christine was at her desk at six, getting her mind fully back into her life's focus. She might be pregnant, she might not be. Either way, her life would only be impacted short-term. She'd continue to take the uterine lining thickening hormone she'd been prescribed, and she'd abstain from wine and fried foods, but otherwise, she had to continue moving forward with her own life. Until her appointment a week from the upcoming Friday—two weeks after implantation—there was absolutely no further reason for her to have contact with Jamie Howe.

She told him so, as gently as she could, when he called.

"At this point, I'm supposed to resume normal activities." She gave him a pretty close rendition of the version she'd rehearsed in the shower that morning.

"I agree..."

"And I might not even have anything of yours living inside me," she interrupted, reminding them both.

"Exactly..."

"We might just be going through the process again next month." She cut in, again.

He could change his mind. Or she could. The contract gave them each that choice. She'd just be required to return the money already deposited in her account.

Which was why she wasn't starting on any major renovations until they heard a heartbeat: roughly six weeks from time of successful implantation.

"So... I'll see you at the doctor's office for the urine test?"

They'd already made the appointment. Together. Friday, by phone from the fertility specialist's office, before the procedure.

"Yes," she said, swallowing disappointment. Did he have to be that eager to have time apart from her?

Show that little interest in seeing her, even once?

Maybe getting to know her a little bit better? After all, she was hopefully going to be carrying his child.

He'd hung up before she could speak further. Or even come to her senses and choose to keep her mouth shut.

Leaving her unusually disgruntled, even a bit put out.

She was a person. With feelings. Not some… Some…

Shaking her head, Christine got up from her desk, heading out to see where she could be of service in the clinic for a few minutes before getting back to the fundraising correspondence. She had an inbox full of responding emails. Had functions to schedule.

Of course she was only a body to Jamie Howe. A machine. She'd known that going in.

It was the only reason she'd agreed to help him in the first place.

But after the weekend… His attention…

Most definitely, they needed the space between them.

Implantation, the beginning of any new project, tended to prompt emotions to run high. Add in the element of the intimacy involved with her part of the process, along with hormonal increases, and it was natural for her to feel a little different than normal.

To begin to accept a familiarity between her and the man whose child she intended to carry. It meant nothing more than that. Wasn't a permanent change in her life. She'd feel the same for Emily Howe, too, were she still alive.

Maybe more so. She could see herself becoming friends with the other woman, had circumstances been different.

And spent that next two weeks training her brain to immediately switch to thoughts of Emily—whose embryo was trying to take root inside of her—anytime she found herself thinking of Jamie. After about ten days of no contact, thoughts of Jamie translated to thoughts of Emily.

Problem solved.

Chapter Nine

Jamie looked at eight houses over the next ten days. He'd had twice that many people going through his home. Every day it became more of an issue to him that he wasn't finding anyplace that felt like home to him.

He had to have a place to go in the event that he got an offer. He was in the process of making a baby and had to have a home for it. His Realtor reminded him that he could take his house off the market and just stay there, but that wasn't an option he wanted to consider. He'd never liked the floor plan of the place. The vaulted ceilings with the upstairs looking down over the living area, made the place feel more like a party house than a home. The house was always too cold upstairs in the winter and too warm in the summer. And when he and Emily had had the backyard surveyed for the pool they'd planned to put in, they'd found that due to city sewer lines, they couldn't dig deeply enough in their backyard in the only area where a pool would have fit.

She'd loved the place. Thought, if nothing else, it would be a great investment. Turned out, it wasn't even that. Due to recent ground settling that had cracked the foundation of a home in the neighborhood, all of the homes in their community had lost value. There was no danger to anyone living in here, but there was the possibility that a homeowner would have the added expense of having to have the home raised and the foundation repaired.

He wasn't going to start a family and then, with single dad duties, also take on moving into a new home. A father provided a home for his children. Gave the child a room that he could grow up in, move away from, and then come back to.

Like Christine's. The place just made you want to walk in the door and stay. Every home he looked at in their exclusive small town failed the "Christine's home" test. It wasn't until his Realtor, after a third frustrating foray out to look at houses, asked him to be more specific in exactly what he wanted that he even realized he'd had a standard.

He was just getting off the phone with the man, finalizing a plan to see three more properties that afternoon, as he pulled into the parking lot of the office building across from the private offices of Christine's ob-gyn.

As though programmed, his gaze immediately searched for her car. Found it parked toward the back of the lot.

Leaving closer spots for those who needed them, he'd guess. He hadn't known the woman long, but could already list several facts that told him she put others' needs in front of her own. The clinic. Her volunteer work. Having his baby.

She wasn't a surrogate who'd put herself on a list. She was doing a favor for him and Emily. On his request.

In deference to the importance of the occasion, he'd put on blue pants with a white polo shirt, instead of jeans or shorts and was glad he'd done so when he caught his first glimpse of Christine. The long, colorful, flowing skirt she had on with a short-sleeved T-shirt would have made him feel underdressed. Every time he'd seen her, even in her home on Sunday, she'd been dressed as though on her way out to some kind of classy lunch with friends at an expensive restaurant.

The outpouring of warmth he felt toward her as he entered the building and saw her standing there by the elevator shook him a bit.

As did his sudden desire to have her standing

there because she'd been waiting for him. Not the elevator.

"You ready for this?" He purposely kept his greeting casual as he approached. She'd made it pretty clear she wanted nothing to do with him other than that which was dictated by their contract.

Since that was all that he wanted, too, all that he needed, all that he'd agreed to, he had no problem with adhering to her stipulations.

"Jamie, hi!" Her smile, when she saw him, wasn't at all casual. At least its effect on him wasn't.

But then, getting ready to find out whether or not he was a father in the making, had him a bit flummoxed.

That had to be all it was. He was about to find out if Emily's baby was on the way.

The elevator bell dinged, the doors opened and they got in together. Both reached for the third floor button at the same time, bumping hands. She dropped hers.

Rather quickly, it seemed to him.

"So…" He held his hands down, clasped in front of him, in the way men did when standing respectfully.

Her lips pressed together, she nodded.

He needed more than that. The contract gave him the right to know medical specifics. Not to know how she was holding up emotionally. Was she still sure she wanted to do this? Having regrets? Okay and ready to go?

Panicked?

"I haven't heard from you so I'm guessing there's been no news…"

Glancing toward the lights showing the movement past the third floor, she said, "I spotted a little bit yesterday."

His stomach dropped. Details were necessary. They'd been told about two kinds of bleeding. One that was common during implantation. The other, a regular monthly cycle, that likely meant no baby.

"I'm sorry. I should have called," she said, glancing at him as the elevator stopped at their floor. "But it wasn't enough to indicate anything, and I knew we were going to be here today…"

They stepped off the elevator, his heart beating a little harder than normal.

"It just felt…a little awkward, you know?" she continued. "Oh, hi, it's Christine Elliott. I just went to the bathroom and saw this… How've the past two weeks been for you?"

Her gaze was open, searching as she pulled him aside. "I've never talked to anyone about my monthly cycle, other than my doctor and the high school nurse when I started the first time. I'm not…"

"Shhh." He shook his head. Aware of far more than he could consciously understand. Aware of her. "It's okay. We're in the learning stages here." Standing against a hallway wall, with doors into office suites around them, he spoke as though there was a microphone nearby. Barely above a whisper. "So... it wasn't like normal monthly stuff?" he asked, as delicately as he could manage.

She shook her head.

"So, do you feel anything?"

"Of course not. It's way too early for that."

He knew. He'd read. Just...

He wasn't ready to go in. Wasn't ready to move past the point of getting started.

Wasn't ready to be disappointed.

"Do you think you might be?" he asked, when what he wanted to do was grill her on her normal monthly cycle. Was she ever late? If so, how often? Did she ever spot first? If so, how much and how often? What kind of chances were they looking at here? How did the data figure into percentages?

With a crook of her head and a small smile she turned toward the door closest to them. "Let's go find out, shall we?"

Jamie followed right behind her.

She'd opted for both urine and blood tests. The first to get an answer quickly, and the second because it was the contractually required confirmation method. Minutes after she'd done both, she sat with Jamie in Dr. Miller's office, waiting for the results.

Jamie was to be present for distribution of all medical information relating to the pregnancy.

He sat unmoving, his hands on his thighs, not even a hint of the finger twitch she'd noticed in her office more than seven weeks before. He hadn't looked at her, or spoken, since he'd entered the office.

She wanted to ask him how he was feeling.

He seemed so alone and someone needed to care.

And then she noticed the wedding band he still wore. And remembered that in his world she wasn't so much a someone as a some*thing*.

That in order to get this job done well, she had to rein in her usual nurturing instincts. She had to quit being motherly to have a baby. She was chuckling inwardly over the irony of that one when the door opened and Cheryl Miller, a woman who'd known her mother and had been the original and sole doctor at The Parent Portal when she'd first opened, walked in.

She knew the second she saw the smile on Cheryl's face what she was going to say and so was looking at Jamie when the doctor spoke.

"Congratulations, Dr. Howe, you're going to be a father!"

His mouth open, he looked immediately at Christine, met her gaze, and for one brief second she felt like the mother of his child. Felt as though they'd just been told they were going to have a baby.

She wanted to jump up. To hug him.

To kiss him long and hard.

Then his gaze dropped reverently to her belly.

And she came to her senses.

"We need to celebrate." Jamie could hardly get a hold of his thoughts as he and Christine exited the doctor's office together. They had a list of dates, future appointments. She had prescriptions that needed to be filled. The plethora of information they'd been given regarding what to expect, what to watch for, when it would be necessary to call the doctor's office—all of it reverberated through his mind, needing to be put on a spreadsheet of some kind.

"No." Christine smiled as she shook her head. "You need to celebrate. I imagine Tom Sanders will be thrilled with the news," she added.

Tom! He hadn't even thought about his father-in-law! Yes, Tom was going to be overjoyed at the prospect of being a grandfather. Even though he didn't think Jamie had made the best decision for himself.

Why hadn't he thought of Tom?

Or worse, why wasn't he thinking of Emily? They'd just reached the culmination of their dreams.

Thanks to the woman walking beside him.

"The blood test results won't be back for a few hours," he told her as they exited the building. "And I've got some houses to look at. How about if we meet at your office right before four?"

Dr. Miller had said she'd call Christine with the results at four.

He was going to be a father.

A *father*. For real. Not just in plans.

She'd stopped just outside the door, standing in the shade of the large awning covering the entryway.

"That's the second time you've mentioned looking at houses."

A statement. Not a question. "I've got my place on the market."

Her frown was unexpected. "You're going through all of this to have the baby you and Emily created, but you're moving from the home you shared with her?"

"I wanted to move from that place when she was alive," he told her, too het up to pay much attention to her remark. "It never felt like a home. And it's dropping in value so isn't a good financial risk, either." He brushed off her questions, wanting first to solidify the location of their four o'clock appointment.

To take her out to a fancy dinner and celebrate their humongous accomplishment. And to make a nonalcoholic toast to the future.

They'd brought an embryo to life.

They were embarking on a partnership. There was so much to talk about. Visitation to discuss. He was to spend time with the baby while in utero so that it would know his voice when it was born, for one thing. Plans to make. Schedules to set.

And all that the doctor had just said about birthing choices. Natural. Epidurals. Assisted. Midwife. Classes.

He was familiar with most of the rhetoric in theory.

In practicality, he knew nothing.

Hadn't discussed any of it with Christine ahead of time, which seemed remiss of him.

"So, your office just before four?" he asked when his thoughts slowed enough to allow him coherent conversation.

She nodded.

"And then dinner?" He'd taken a step toward the parking lot. She was right beside him. "We can go out," he said, hearing the supersonic energy in his voice. Hoped he didn't sound as frenetic to her as it felt to him. "Nothing personal. Just business. We have so much to discuss…"

When he glanced at her, she was grinning. And nodding. "Fine. We can go out. But Jamie…"

"Yeah?"

"Call your father-in-law. You shouldn't be celebrating this alone."

He wasn't alone.

He was with her.

But she wasn't celebrating.

She was doing a job.

Chapter Ten

With hands that were shaking for no good reason, Christine pulled out her phone the second she was in her car, checking for pertinent emails or voice messages that might have come through during the time her phone had been on silent.

There'd been a few of both. Important, but not urgent.

And Olivia had texted. Her friend had been heading into court but wanted to know the results.

Positive, she typed back, and dropped her phone into the pocket on the side of her brightly colored bag.

This wasn't life-changing news for her, just life altering for a short period of time.

The baby wasn't even hers.

She started her car, pulled out into traffic, thought about the emails she'd briefly skimmed. The voice messages she'd sort of heard.

Wondered if Jamie had called Tom.

Hoped he had. Now Jamie was one who'd just had life-changing news. He'd been so happy he'd almost been irritatingly talkative.

Except that she'd found his uncharacteristic lack of focus endearing...

The man really wanted this baby.

Such a great thing.

Men wanted children. She saw it every day in her business. So why was she glomming on to the way his eyes had glistened in that first second after the announcement? On the almost uncontainable energy coursing through him so quickly he couldn't seem to rein himself in?

Why did it hurt so badly that a man was feeling that way about a baby *she* was carrying?

No. She wasn't going there.

This most definitely wasn't about her.

And that fact made it much more difficult to smile at the barrage of faces entering her office, sometimes in duplicate, on and off for the rest of that afternoon. Her full-time staff of seven, the doctors who worked for them, the technicians who were assigned by their employer labs to clinic, even the crew from the cleaning company, one by one, came in to either hear the test results, or to congratulate her because they had heard them.

She smiled. Thanked them all for their support. And reminded every single one of them that Jamie Howe was the one deserving of congratulations.

The baby was his. Not hers.

Still in his dress pants and polo shirt, Jamie appeared at her office door at five minutes before four. The way she reacted to the sight of that athletic body with that dark hair tipping his collar, and the hazel gaze meeting hers, you'd think the man meant something to her. Personally.

She almost walked from behind her desk to give him a hug.

It was just the emotion of the day, she knew that, mixed in with a bit of hormonal fluctuation. Now that she was pregnant, her body, and prenatal vitamins, would be naturally producing everything her uterus needed, so she was to stop the fertility medication. It wouldn't stop the roller coaster of emotions, though. She'd forgotten that from the past.

Jamie had barely said hello and mentioned that he might have found a house, when Cheryl rang in. Putting the phone on speaker, Christine and Jamie listened together as the doctor said that the blood test confirmed what they already knew.

And reminded them that their due date was March 14.

Cheryl congratulated Jamie again, reminded Christine to call her anytime before her next appointment if she had any issues and hung up, leaving them standing there on opposite sides of her desk, looking at each other.

So much was going on inside her, both physically and emotionally. She struggled for words. Knew she had to find them.

She was the professional. Jamie was paying for her services, yes, but he was, in essence, a client. One not associated with the clinic for legal purposes, but still a client.

It was up to her to take charge.

"What time did you want to meet for dinner?"

Not quite the business discussion she'd thought to have. But that's why they were having dinner. To discuss business.

"March 14 is good." Jamie dropped to the chair in front of her desk. "You won't be heavily pregnant during the heat of the summer."

She nodded. Had already figured that into the plan before she'd been impregnated. And said, "March 14 is a bit long to wait for dinner."

He grinned. "Dinner can be whenever you want. This might be way too soon, but I've been thinking all afternoon about what Dr. Miller said about the actual birth," he said then. "We'll need to schedule classes, depending on which way we go." He was like an eager student as he looked over at her. She could almost see his mind racing. There was nothing personal in the look. He was just all in with the news he'd received.

Her heart warmed as she sat, too. And while she didn't have long, with another appointment due in fifteen minutes, she figured it was better to have this part of the discussion in her office. With a desk between them. Not in some restaurant where the staff mistook them for a couple.

"Obviously you have all the say on this one," he was saying, sitting forward with knees spread and his elbows on the arms of his chair.

Forcing her gaze away from his face, his chest, she shook her head. Looked at a gestational calendar on her desk. She kept it on hand for discussions with clients, but had pulled it out that afternoon to remind herself, in a businesslike manner, what lay ahead for her now that she knew her body was going to produce a child.

"You have a say, too," she said. "Some things are slightly riskier than others. Like home birthing, which I'm going to say right now is not my preference, unless you and Emily had some reason for wanting it that way. I know that a lot of couples are doing the bathtub birthing process, with good results, but since I'm not going to be bonding with the baby…"

She wasn't thinking about her body naked. She was merely discussing a human function.

"Of course not," he said immediately, clasping his hands. "I'm seriously fine with whatever you think. I didn't realize, until Dr. Miller said so, that more women are actually choosing C-section births…"

"Again, I'd rather not," she said. "If it's necessary for my health or that of the baby then, of course, but if not…"

She'd rather not have to deal with the recovery time. Or carry a scar as a reminder for the rest of her life. Although, to be reminded of the gift she was giving someone else shouldn't be a bad thing. With Ryder she'd pushed him out and had been up and moving around within hours. Had been home the next day.

"So, I guess, if all goes normally, we've decided on natural childbirth," he said, cocking his head slightly as he looked over at her.

She was going to have his baby. And he'd be there. Witnessing one of the most intimate moments of her life. Coaching her through the process.

Something happened when her gaze met his. Something electric. Warm. Compelling.

And not at all appropriate.

Jamie didn't want to leave her office. Not even for the hour and a half before they met up again at a restaurant on Main Street.

They'd just embarked on a collaborative venture that was changing his whole world. They were creating life—him with his embryos and her with the capability of turning a microscopic piece of genetics into a human being. He couldn't quite wrap his mind around the news. He just knew that she was a major component of it.

And knew that she'd always be a significant part of his child's life. Whether she ever wanted contact or not. She was the birth mother.

The child wouldn't exist without her. That mattered.

He called his Realtor. Told him to put in a full price offer on the home he'd found. A two-story in a quiet, gated neighborhood with a big yard, it was across the street from the ocean. He didn't call Tom.

Not yet.

He went for a run, instead. To work off some of the excess energy coursing through him. Late afternoon in June wasn't the best time to be running on the beach. Dodging kids and buckets and half-buried plastic shovels made the activity a challenge. He welcomed every obstacle. Every child in his path. That father half lying in the sand, covered with the raspy granules, next to his toddler, building a mound, would be him in a couple of years. The one dodging waves with a grade-schooler—him, too. His feet plodded in the sand as sweat trickled down his bare back and into the waistband of the black swimsuit he'd put on.

For two years he'd been coasting. That stopped

that day. The next stage of his life was upon him. Opening a future filled with new activity. New adventures.

New challenges.

He was up for every one of them.

He ran hard. Farther than normal. Trying to decide which of the three bedrooms upstairs in the new house, in addition to the master, would be best for a nursery. The one closest to him made the most sense. But it was smaller and on the east side of the house, which meant sun every single day. A lot of the day. Might be too hot. The one at the opposite end of the hall had only one northern exposure window. But it was too far away. And purple. He'd have to paint, multiple times, before buying furniture.

The one in the middle had an odd alcove in it to make room for the shower in the hall bathroom. And the closet in there was miniscule. Wouldn't matter so much when his little one was a baby, but as it grew…

He picked up his pace, careful to keep enough distance between his feet spewing sand and beach patrons. Rooms, decorating weren't his specialties. They'd been Emily's. And critical to making a house into a home. *Otherwise you just had a building with stuff in it*, Emily used to say.

The building mattered, too, he'd tried to tell her. The house they'd bought had had her touches, but still hadn't felt like home.

But without her touches, would the new house feel like one?

They'd been so good together because, other than buying the house, they'd always found solutions that came from both of them. Their differences, their strengths, had complemented each other, and only together had they found the perfect whole.

He'd given in on the house, though they'd both eventually realized the mistake of his having done so. And Emily had loved the place. He wasn't sure he'd have moved her away from it.

One thing was for sure, he was glad they'd bought it. That she'd lived out her last years in a place she'd loved.

Slowing, he stepped hard in the sand for a few steps, his velocity trying to carry him as his legs were stopping.

What in the hell was he doing?

Breathing hard, he leaned over, his hands on his knees.

He and Emily had made embryos so that they could raise a child, have a family, together. Both of them—each contributing their differences, their strengths, to a happy, healthy result. Making up for each other's shortcomings. Having each other's backs.

He couldn't even figure out which room to put the crib in without her.

How had he possibly thought he could raise their child alone?

Sitting down, he faced the ocean, forearms resting on raised knees.

We're having a baby. He looked toward the setting sun.

And started to calm. Watching the horizon, its endlessness. Waves that continued to move. Day and night. Always. Without stopping. Ever.

Like the love he shared with Emily.

We're having a baby.

He wasn't doing it alone. He was doing it differently than he and Em had imagined, but she'd be there. In the genetics of the child they'd created together. A child that would bring parts of Emily into their new home. Perhaps making up for some of his failings.

And if not, they'd still be fine.

"We're having a baby," he said out loud, softly, just enough to hear his voice. To know it was real.

Maybe it was staring toward the sun that brought tears to his eyes. Maybe it was the acute loneliness and the love he still felt for his wife.

Maybe it was gratitude for what life was bringing to him.

All he knew for sure was that he had to cancel dinner.

And call Tom.

He and Emily were having a baby.

Chapter Eleven

Jamie called Christine every day, just checking in. The calls were short, never more than a minute, and just him asking her how she was feeling. He didn't ask anything about her personal life, and didn't offer anything from his. He never said why he'd canceled dinner that Friday and she didn't ask. Presumed he'd been with his father-in-law. And knew in her heart that that was how it should be.

She'd cried herself to sleep that night, though, her hand cradling her belly. Just an overload of various emotions that needed to be expended. And then she got on with the business of growing a healthy baby.

With Cheryl's permission she was back to play-ing racquetball—though being careful not to hit a ball so hard it came back and hit her in the stomach. Exercise within reason was not only healthy for the baby, but would help her have an easier delivery, too. She went to bed an hour earlier every night, and if she couldn't sleep, at least she was resting.

And she heard Gram's voice every time she put a bite in her mouth, reminding her that what she ate, her baby ate. Gram had been willing to let her keep Ryder. Had been willing to have a crying baby in the house, to release some of Christine's trust money to support it. Gramps had been on board as well. And for a few months there, the first few months, she'd actually allowed herself to believe that she could keep her baby. She'd fallen in love with her son.

And yet she'd done the absolute right thing in giving him up. She'd loved him too much to force him to grow up with less than what adult parents could give him. And she'd loved Gram and Gramps too much to cut short their last years of life. With both of them in failing health, the stress of having a baby in the house would have killed them.

The choice to make the adoption private, without contact, had been her father's. He'd thought it best that she rip off the bandage, as he'd put it. That she be forced to forget about Ryder as best she could and get on with her life. She'd "gotten on" to The Parent Portal, where there was always a choice for contact.

And Jamie was allowing her contact. She thought about Jamie a lot. Because it was his baby growing inside her. How could she not? He wasn't hers, just as the baby wasn't hers, but there was something very intimate about having his seed alive inside her.

His and Emily's.

She struggled to keep the other woman in the forefront of her mind. The baby was Emily's as much as it was Jamie's.

But she'd only met Emily once. Christine had some key memories, but could only play them so many times over and over without anything new to add.

She was ready for Jamie's call Monday morning—between seven and eight, as they'd been the previous two days—prepared to tell him that she'd slept well, and everything else was status quo. She figured, after a week or so, his calls would cut back to every other day. And then maybe every three or four. He didn't have to call at all. Or see her. The level of contact had been left up to him.

She'd gone into the process knowing that she could do it on her own. And be just fine. She'd have her monthly checkups, do what she was told, and grow his baby for him.

"I had an offer on my house over the weekend," he told her, instead of wishing her a good day and hanging up after her report. "Closing is set for a week after my new place closes, so everything's going to work out on that end."

In her office, she sat back in her chair, studying

the pattern of ridges on her black, short-sleeved shirt. And then how those ridges lined up with the blue, white, black and purple flowers on her cotton skirt. She didn't love the colors. But the skirt was soft. And she loved how it flowed around her when she walked.

Jamie's housing situation was none of her concern. None of her business. Her clothes were. Still, she had clients tell her things about their nonbaby personal lives now and then. She was being too rigid.

"Congratulations!" she said. "Everything in your life seems to be coming together, Jamie. I'm happy for you."

The words were 1,000 percent true. And felt good.

"I was just letting you know that I've taken care of my immediate responsibilities and would like to set up a visitation schedule."

Oh. Oh! No. Just *oh*. She calmed the jump of excitement in her stomach. "Okay. What did you have in mind?"

"How much can you stand having me around?"

She wasn't even going to let her mind contemplate the answer to that one. "Seriously," she said. "Do you have some ideas of what you're looking for?"

"If I had my way, we'd see each other every day," he told her. "But I also realize you have a life to live and I'm not a part of that. I know the sacrifice you're making for me. I just…forgive me, but you've got my whole future there and it's hard to not be present all the time."

Her heart melted. For him. For her. Because she didn't hate the idea of seeing him every day.

"We said in the contract that you could be," she told him. The man had just found out that a part of his wife lived on. This wasn't about her.

Why did she have to keep reminding herself of that?

Maybe because, in the moment, her whole life was being disrupted. So, yeah, she was allowed a bit of having it be about her.

"I generally work twelve-hour days during the week," she told him. "But I take breaks for some exercise and other things that come up. We could choose a time to meet a few times a week." He wanted every day. The fact that she wasn't opposed to that much contact with him told her that it probably wasn't a good idea.

"I was thinking something a little more flexible," he said. It sounded like he was moving around. She'd pictured him in his car. On his way to… Where?

"Where are you?"

"Walking on the beach. I just finished a run."

An immediate picture of his strong thighs, his tight and perfectly shaped backside, came to mind. She shouldn't have asked. Had had no valid reason to do so.

And had to figure out how she was going to make this work. Seeing him. And yet not seeing-seeing him.

"Okay, so more flexible. You want to just play it

by ear? Call when you have a minute and see if I'm free?" She wasn't going to be in about five minutes since she had an appointment.

Yes. Think about work, about others… That had always been her panacea.

"I'm fine with setting up dates. I'd just like to vary the times of day, and the days of the week if we could. You know, so the baby hears my voice throughout the day, or, at least, hears it at night sometimes, in the morning sometimes…"

It made perfect sense. This baby wasn't going to have a mother. It most definitely deserved all the help she could give it bonding with its father.

When she realized she was cradling her flat stomach again with her free hand, feeling the same kind of ownership she'd felt with Ryder, she sat up to her desk.

Concentrated on the issue at hand. Being more flexible fit her better. She lived a fluid life. Told Jamie so. And offered to be free that evening to further discuss.

Somehow, in the hours in between, she was going to have to figure out a way not to like him and his baby quite so much. How to care for the baby without caring—caring for it.

The situation was understandably emotional. But those emotions were situation based, not lifelong commitments.

She was the professional here. The one doing a

job. So it was up to her to keep the situation from spiraling out of control. To remember that he'd hired her body.

Not her heart.

Christine called just before five to say that she'd have an hour in between work and an evening commitment and he was welcome to drop by her place for their chat.

"I'm actually at the college of art here in town, in the middle of hanging art on the walls of the classroom. Can you meet me here?" he asked. And then added, "I thought maybe it would be good if you could visit me in my world, maybe once a week at least, if that works for you, so that the baby becomes familiar with the surroundings." It all sounded slightly hooey to him, but he'd read a lot about the importance of environment during pregnancy. Professionals in the field seemed to pretty much agree that babies were affected, at least somewhat, by things that went on outside the womb during their gestation.

Even if it didn't help, it couldn't hurt.

Christine had agreed immediately, and he was outside in the parking lot, waiting to lead her into the building that housed his classroom and small office. While classes hadn't yet started, first year students were moving into dorms, preparing for orientation, so the campus had a sense of life about it. His building was completely empty, though, and he let them in with his security card.

He'd seen her just three days before, and yet it was all brand-new again, the sense of life picking up when she was around.

Because she was carrying his child. He knew that his attraction to her was because she was pregnant with his baby. Just like he'd have felt a new and energized attraction for Emily had she lived and was the one bringing their family to life. It was natural.

But that skirt she was wearing—purple, black and blue little flowers on a white background—the way those flowers molded her, flowed around her calves with every step she took...

He pulled at the hem of the T-shirt covering the blue shorts he'd put on, making sure that it covered any evidence of how much he liked that skirt. And the ribbed top... It was sinful, really, the way the fabric outlined those breasts so perfectly. Hugged them so softly.

The way he was reacting to her was sinful. One thought of the child who would be setting up his classroom with him the following year—probably in a swaddle attached to his body—and he had himself under control.

"So what are we doing here?"

With a shard of guilt spearing through him, he turned to look at Christine. Oh God, if she'd seen, or sensed... He wasn't a creepy guy. Didn't ever get

all het up over the mere sight of a woman. Not even
Emily. He saw younger women, with great bodies
and far fewer clothes, pretty much every day during his run on the beach. Found them attractive, of
course. He was human. But he didn't struggle to keep
his reaction to them under control.

Generally, his body just minded its manners on
its own.

Christine wasn't looking at him at all. She'd
picked up one of the several pieces of art lying along
a bookshelf that lined one whole wall of the classroom.

"I teach math to art students," he told her. "Right
brain, left brain. Opposite ends of the spectrum, to
some. But in reality, art and math are encompass-
ing visual depictions of the universe around us…"

He stopped. Emily used to glaze over when he got
his Math on. As did a lot of people. "Sorry," he said.
"I forget sometimes that numbers, measurements,
spatial science and the way they all depict the world
isn't all that exciting to the general population."

She'd moved to a canvas with geometrical shapes.
On the surface that's what it was. If you stepped back
and looked at the colors, you'd see a face there. And
a single tear. "I'm intrigued."

"I use art to teach mathematical concepts," he
said. "Or rather, I challenge my students to use their
art to show me the concepts I'm teaching them. I'm
not an artist. At all. These were all final exams."

"So, your students did these?"

She'd stopped at a three-dimensional, digitally printed plastic dollhouse.

"Last semester. The top grades from all of my classes. I display them for the following semester, use them actually, as teaching tools when I'm introducing concepts, and then the students get them back."

She'd stopped at the poster-board-sized colored pencil drawing showing exponential math through pictures. A big bear with three little bears to show the concept of something cubed. There were thirty drawings in all. The bottom one showed an entire equation complete with solution through children's pictures.

"This was a math education class, geared for art students who want to teach middle schoolers," he said. He was standing close to point out a couple of the students' impressive highlights and caught a sniff of… Something flowery. Deliciously so. And stepped back. Quickly. The arm that he'd had outstretched to point to a part of the drawing brushed against her breast in his haste.

His brain froze. Did he apologize? Draw attention to the flame she seemed to ignite within him? Or pretend it hadn't happened, that it was no big deal?

"What's this one?" She'd moved on to an abstract piece and he had to struggle to come up with the mathematical concept found within it. Throughout it.

His blunder was no big deal. He had to see that his reaction to her stayed that way.

No big deal.

Chapter Twelve

She had herself in check. Had almost forgotten her core purpose when she'd leaned in a little too close to Jamie as he was showing her math in abstract art and he'd brushed against her, but she'd moved away. Moved on. Kept her mind on the job at hand.

Giving Jamie and his unborn child exposure to each other, helping them build the bond that would last them a lifetime and beyond.

It didn't take a lot of effort. No heavy conversation or soul-searching required. Just being physically present with her belly in his space. She helped him hang and display all of the artwork on his shelf in less than half an hour.

"Wow, thanks," he said, standing back with her to

view the results. "Seriously, this would have taken me a couple of hours or more, and the results would not have been so aesthetically pleasing," he said.

She chuckled at his self-deprecatory tone. "Aesthetically pleasing?" she asked. "Doesn't sound like a Dr. Howe comment."

He'd been grinning, too, but his expression sobered at her words. "Emily said it a lot," he said, his mood noticeably changed. Subtly. But still noticeable. It was like a fan had been turned off. Leaving the air in the room stale.

Going to the desk at the front of the room, he gathered tape and nails, a hammer and some tacks together and locked them in a file cabinet in the corner.

"It's okay to talk about her, you know. In fact, I think it's best if you do." It's what she would tell any couple in her office, facing their situation. Along with telling him to seek counseling, except that she knew he'd already done so.

As had she. Before she'd signed on to be his surrogate. And she'd go back if she ever came up against a struggle she couldn't handle.

Half sitting on the corner of one of the student desks in the front row, Christine folded her arms and let him see the compassion she felt for him. As she did with most of her clients. Her compassion was what she had to give.

He faced her, his bottom half mostly hidden behind his desk. The light seemed to have dimmed in his expression and she wished life had been kinder to him.

Reminded herself that it was about to get much better, but harder, too, as he faced the challenges involved in raising a child alone.

He straightened. Nodded. Put his hands on his desk in front of him. Like he was ready to make a point.

"I'm struggling a bit here, unexpectedly," he said, looking her right in the eye. As though trying to impart a particular message. "I think it's only fair, given the unusual circumstances between us, that you know."

She nodded, too. "Yes. That's good. Talk it out. We knew this wasn't going to be easy. Only that for you it would be worth it." A thought occurred to her, along with a stab of horror that left as quickly as it came. Still… "You do still feel that way, don't you? That it's worth it? You want this baby, right?"

If not, there'd be a family that did, she reminded herself. Lists of couples with loving homes, waiting to fill them with children, were miles long.

The instant sense of protectiveness that had come over her regarding the baby inside her was not altogether new. But it was a not quite welcome regurgitation of days long past. If he didn't want the baby, could she think about keeping it?

Could she make herself give up a second child to strangers?

"Of course I want my baby!" Jamie's stern, wide-eyed expression, his commanding tone left her in no doubt as to the truth of his words. "I admit to experiencing some unexpected emotional ups and downs here, but none of them, not a single one, have anything to do with wanting that baby. I did. I do. I always will."

Good. She nodded. Okay then, they were fine.

"The struggle I was referring to has to do with you."

Not fine? They weren't done here. "Me? Am I doing something that displeases you? If so, you definitely need to speak up. That's why we have the contract, to protect both sides. If you have a problem…"

His head shake stopped her words.

"You aren't going to get something like this to fit neatly into a contract," he told her. "I'm just…you're carrying my child…you went from a virtual stranger to…the woman carrying my child. There are feelings involved with that…and…and… God, I feel like a first-class ass, and…"

She recognized guilt when she heard it. Her heart softened. Opened a bit more.

"Jamie. It's fine," she told him, wanting to help him feel better. "I promise you it's perfectly natural that you'd feel some resentment toward me. Emily, your wife, the woman you've loved since you were eight, should be carrying this child. Not me. You can't help but have a part of you resent that…"

There were some things you just couldn't fix. But you could make them more bearable by sitting with those who were suffering. Offering comfort.

"It's not resentment I'm feeling." He was still standing straight. The intensity of his gaze hadn't lessened in the least.

"It's not?"

"No."

Her mouth was dry. She no longer wanted to continue the conversation.

"I'm finding myself attracted to you," he said. "We hardly know each other. But...you're carrying my child. The most important part of me is inside you, dependent upon you, and...like I said, I'm a first-class ass."

She shook her head again, tried to shore up the walls around her feelings. "It's just a product of the situation," she told him. Knowing that, above all else, to keep things professional, ethical, safe, she could not allow her own feelings to come into the situation.

She'd be betraying his trust if she did so.

And if she acted unprofessionally, she could do damage to the clinic's reputation as well.

"A form of transference, and completely understandable," she said, with a little too much breathlessness for her liking, as the words came to her. "Certainly nothing to beat yourself up about," she added, finding strength from within to give them both a solid piece of advice.

"You're not an ass, Jamie. You're a decent man who's owned up to something that you could have just kept secret. Which makes this situation safer for both of us. What we're doing here is a beautiful thing, a miracle, really, but with every great thing there's a shadow side, too. By nature of all that's involved, pregnancy, even a planned and traditional one, generates a lot of varying emotion. Nothing's free. We'll get through this…"

The words were powerful. She felt them. Saw his face relax and allowed relief to flow through her as he grinned. Nodded.

"I'm sure you're right," he said as he turned off the office lights and locked the door behind him.

They walked silently, side by side, several inches between them, out to the parking lot.

He stopped by her car, and she turned to ask him when he wanted to meet again.

"I do see real truth in what you said," he told her, just inches away, his gaze locked with hers as though he had some otherworldly mesmerizing power. "But you are a beautiful woman, Christine. I'd notice you whether you were carrying my baby or not."

Notice her. Like he probably noticed most women of an appropriate age, as men did.

"Jamie…"

He held up a hand. "Don't worry, I'm not hitting on you. I'm just keeping it all out in the open, as you said."

He could have been hitting on her. They were alone in a deserted parking lot with the sun setting romantically behind them.

But he wasn't. She believed him. One hundred percent.

And that didn't stop her body from wishing that he had been.

That he could be.

That she could lean in and touch her lips to his.

But of course, she didn't say so.

She wasn't going to get weak and blow this.

Too much was at stake.

The next several days settled into a routine of sorts. Jamie ran every morning. Worked with his tennis team most afternoons during the week. Started two of his online classes. Drove up to the university in Mission Viejo to his campus office to attend meetings and prepare for classes there that were due to start after Labor Day. He had dinner with Tom a couple of times.

And had dinner with Axel and his mother, Sandra, once, too. She'd made steak tartare. Was a great cook. A good mother. And an immensely attractive woman who did absolutely nothing for him. He enjoyed the evening. Figured, when she said they'd do it again sometime, that he'd accept that invitation.

He didn't tell them, or anyone in his life other than Tom, that he was going to be a father. Things were still so new. So private. He wanted to savor the news for himself, not answer questions about the somewhat unusual choice he'd made.

Which meant that, other than the brief time spent with Tom, the only time he could really be himself, live the life that was coursing through him, was during his visits with Christine. With his baby.

They had them regularly in various locations and during different times of day, and he got through everything else on his schedule just to get to those visits. Christine had been right. Bringing out his attraction to her, naming it for the transference it was, made things much easier between them. They'd been to the grocery store once, just chatting as they walked up and down the aisles together with their own baskets, each doing their own shopping. When they both reached for the same box of bran cereal, they might have touched hands, but he saved them from the collision just in time. He let her have the first box and took the second for himself.

A couple of days later they met at a bagel shop midmorning, for a quick snack. She liked her bagels plain with butter. He was a cream cheese guy all the way.

The Sunday after her visit to his classroom, they took a walk on the beach. He'd hesitated before suggesting that particular outing. The beach was a constant in his life, a part of every day, which meant that it would play an important role in his child's life as well and should be familiar.

It was also the place where he felt closest to Emily.

A place he reserved in his mind for just the two of them.

Needing Emily to be as much a part of their baby's life as possible was what eventually convinced him to suggest that Christine join him there. She was attending a fundraising cruise later that day, but had agreed to meet him just after sunrise. In his running shorts, T-shirt and tennis shoes, he waited for her at the parking lot to the Marie Cove resident public beach entrance.

And glanced away when his body immediately reacted to the feminine thighs shaped softly by the black capri yoga pants she had on. The colorful mid-length sport top that outlined a stomach still completely firm and flat didn't help.

With a flip-flop in each hand, she walked up barefoot to tell him hello.

Maybe he should have run first, so he'd be smelly and not feeling at all sexy when she met his gaze and smiled.

An easy smile.

An understanding one?

As soon as they were on the sand, it seemed suddenly mandatory that he tell Christine that he sometimes talked to his deceased wife as he ran.

"Did she run with you?"

"No," he said as he noticed a series of little bird tracks left in the sand. Something he didn't generally see as he ran. "She was always a bike rider. When we were in high school, she'd ride her bike and I'd run alongside her."

"You didn't like riding?"

"I did. I still do. We used to take day, and half-day rides. I just prefer running for daily exercise."

"I hate exercising."

The news kind of pleased him. Seemed to put more of a separation between the two of them in real life, as if the only things they had in common were bran cereal and the baby she was carrying for him.

"Which is why I play racquetball."

That was in the tennis family. He left the comment alone in his mind.

"So tell me about her," she said next, seeming to understand that Emily was the reason he'd suggested the outing. Understanding him with him saying so very little.

Twenty minutes later, after having regaled her with various memories that had popped into his mind—their first dance at their wedding when she'd started to cry because she was so happy to finally be married to him; the time they'd sneaked out of town to go on a date without anyone knowing they were together, only to run into another judge who worked with her father; the entire Saturday they'd spent decorating Christmas cookies with his mother—he wasn't feeling any closer to Emily.

Christine was still there with him, though, his awareness of her a palpable thing.

"I looked you and Emily up in the high school yearbook," she said softly. "I don't remember either one of you from when I was in school, but it's clear she was pretty popular."

"Everyone loved her." And she'd chosen him. "But that's because she was so easy to like. Emily was just one of those people who was comfortable in her own skin and so made others so. She had a way of taking things in stride, seeing the best in people."

He was making her sound like a saint. In her own way, she had been. He'd loved her deeply. And maybe he'd wished that she'd been a little less easygoing when it came to her time. To always being ready to help out, leaving them so little time alone together. Or so it had seemed to him.

"So why did you need to sneak out of town to go on a date?"

He shrugged. Kicked up some sand with his tennis shoe. Noticed Christine's bare toes. He couldn't picture Emily's. Wasn't sure he'd ever noticed them. Knew for certain he'd never found them the least bit sexy.

What was sexy about toes?

Maybe it was the red polish.

A date. She'd asked about why he and Emily

had kept their relationship a secret. Seemed so long ago—a completely different world. When in reality, the two of them had shared their first kiss right on that same beach.

"There were people who thought that I wasn't good enough for Emily. This town…with all its Beverly Hills types…her father being a judge…the country club…she was raised in that world, vacationed with those families, spent weekends on yachts. Had a full ride to college before she was born. I lived in a two-bedroom house across town from the beach, would only get to college on student loans, if then, and the only vacations we took were when we went camping." He told it like it was.

"And somehow you say that without sounding like a victim. Or sorry for yourself."

"Because I don't." The response was immediate. "I might not have grown up with monetary riches, but I never doubted that my life was filled with wealth."

"Even though your dad was sick?" she asked.

For a second there he'd forgotten that he'd told her about the emergency room visit when he was eight. The day he'd met Emily.

"He was my dad. We played sports together. He taught me how to catch fish. Did everything other families around us did. His kidney problem was just something that he dealt with. It wasn't like it defined him or our family. He wouldn't let it slow him down—other than the times he was in renal failure, and even then, he was always certain he'd be fine and wanted to know everything that was going on with me. Keeping track of things. Holding me accountable. Encouraging me. I never felt like he wasn't there for me. He lived his life, rather than making a life out of being sick. He did what he wanted to do, almost until the day he died."

"He sounds like a great guy." The words could have been placating. Polite. Instead, they sounded wistful, like she was sorry she hadn't gotten to know him.

"Emily was kind of uncomfortable around him." He was surprised to hear the words come out of his mouth. Hadn't even been aware of thinking them.

"Why?" Christine didn't look over at him. Or sound judgmental. She'd been watching the sand pretty much since they'd stepped out on it.

Looking for treasure? Or for hidden pitfalls to avoid with bare skin?

He didn't have an answer. Wasn't even sure why he'd made the statement. "I think she just felt so sorry for him. Her dad was so larger than life and mine…spent months at a time getting healthy enough to just go camping again."

"I think that makes him larger than life," Christine said softly. "He certainly lived larger than most would have with his life."

She hadn't stepped any nearer to him. He hadn't moved over, either.

And yet Jamie felt closer to her than ever before.

Chapter Thirteen

She'd wanted to kiss him. They'd been standing there on the beach and she'd almost leaned in... knowing that, Christine should not have taken pity on Jamie, with all the packing he had to do. He was a big boy. Could tape and load boxes. There'd been no reason for her offer to help him. Christine knew, as soon as she'd heard herself make the offer as they left each other at their vehicles on Sunday, that she'd been out of line. Which was why she cringed when she saw Olivia's name come up on her caller ID the following Tuesday just as she was walking in the door from work. She had ten minutes to change into shorts and a T-shirt and get back out the door. Jamie was bringing enchiladas home for them to share before they got busy.

And Olivia would be calling to ask Christine to stand in for her that night at the center.

Olivia knew she could count on Christine as backup. And vice versa. More often the former, since Christine's job didn't often involve life and death emergencies.

"Hey there!" she answered with forced cheer. "What's up?"

"What's wrong?"

"Nothing. Just in a hurry to get changed." She didn't have to say why. She was busy. Olivia was busy. They didn't report in to each other with every move they made. Which was partially why they worked so well as friends.

"I'm rushing, too. I'm standing in for Mary in the kitchen before card class, but I just wanted to tell you, I saw Judge Sanders when I was at the country club for lunch today. Someone said the hottie he was with was his son-in-law."

"You saw Jamie?" Dr. Howe, dammit. Whatever she called him in private, to everyone else she knew him as Dr. Howe.

"Jamie?" Olivia said the word slowly. "You're calling a business associate, Dr. Jamison Howe, Jamie? Christine, what are you doing?"

"He's going to be in my hip pocket for the next

eight months," she reminded. "Coming to my doctor's appointments. He asked me to call him Jamie."

The pause made her uncomfortable. "You're sure this is a good idea? Spending so much time with the guy."

They'd already been through that particular discussion to the satisfaction of both of them, she'd thought. Which had helped her calm down over her growing feelings for Jamie.

"You were the one who confirmed that studies showed that babies could hear in utero. And that bonding with the father was particularly beneficial in this case."

"I know. And as a doctor, I do believe it's important. As your friend...hearing the way you just said his name... I just don't want you to get hurt."

She didn't want to get hurt, either. "My walls are up and fortified," she assured her friend. "Besides, you know me. I'm not looking for a relationship. Don't even want one. And guys like Jamie...they're made for them. I need my independence. My freedom to work twelve-hour days and spend time at the center and have drinks with you..."

No need to discuss the fact that she had the hots for her client/employer. Or that he'd told her he was attracted to her. She'd had hormone shots before she'd conceived. And now that she was pregnant, her body was producing more of them. That explained her increased libido. Just like the transference that he was suffering from.

None of it was real.

They just had to keep their eyes on the bigger picture.

"Welcome to the mess," Jamie greeted her, holding what looked like a piece of framed wall art, as he pulled open the front door at the address he'd given her. "Dinner's on warm in the oven, so we can eat first and then pack, or do some packing first."

In navy running shorts and a T-shirt, framed by cathedral ceilings and an expensive-looking light brown leather couch and love seat behind him, the man looked...melt her insides gorgeous.

"Let's do some packing first," she said in spite of the fact that she was kind of hungry. It was best to stay busy during the time she brought his baby visiting. And most important that she be occupied at that moment. Stepping into his home, even with things out of place and boxes lining one wall, gave her a much more personal sense of him.

She was already carrying his baby. She didn't need to get any more personal. "You said you were most intimidated by the china and glassware, so why don't I start in the kitchen?"

He'd mentioned his packing woes as they'd parted ways at their cars at the beach on Sunday. "Actually,

I was hoping you'd help me out in the bedroom," he said.

Her gaze flew toward his, eyes open wide, heart pounding. He'd already turned away, was settling the frame in his hand, backside out, against a wall. "The closet and drawers are filled with Emily's things," he said. "I had no idea what to do with them and it was just easier to leave them where they were, but you've mentioned this women's center you volunteer at. I like that the people in need earn spending dollars by taking classes to better themselves, and then spend them in the center's shop for things they need. I'd like you to take a look at Emily's things and see if you think women at the center can use them."

How a heart could change gears so quickly, she didn't know, but Christine was no longer suffering from inappropriate sexual needs. Instead, she'd just grown a little fonder of the man inside that incredible body as she followed him up the open staircase.

"You sure you want me in here, doing this?" Christine stood in Emily's walk-in closet, directly across the little hallway from the closed door of his identical in design clothes storage room. His was a bit less packed. The hallway, of sorts, was a small walkway of tile between the master bedroom and the attached huge room that had two full vanities with sinks and mirrors on opposite sides, with a garden tub and separate double shower. Another door led off to a small room that set the toilet off from the rest of the suite.

It had all been a bit much for him when they moved in. Who needed so much wasted floor space in the middle of a bathroom? It did nothing but hold a rug and collect hair. It wasn't like you were ever going to plop down there and play a game or watch TV.

But you could dance there with your wife... The memory came and he let it wash over him. The day he and Emily had first looked at the house, he'd told her straight out he didn't like it, had complained about the waste of square footage in the master bath. She'd pulled him against her right there in the middle of the room, pressing her hips against his and starting to sway. Humming the song they'd danced their first dance to the night of their wedding.

He hadn't been all that fond of the song, either. But she'd loved it.

And he'd loved her...

"Hey, do you want..." Christine's voice was muffled and then not as she came out of the closet. "What's wrong?"

He shook his head. Glanced at her and felt the melancholy fade. "Nothing. Just thinking about how much there is to do..."

"If you aren't ready to get rid of her things, just say so, Jamie. We can pack them up and you can store them..."

Because to hang them in the new house would just be weird.

Thing was, he didn't even want to.

He was ready to get rid of them.

And felt like crap for feeling that way.

Moving on from grief was not for lightweights.

"I'm ready," he told her. And added, "I wasn't, but I am now."

Standing in the doorway of the closet, he watched as Christine moved hangers along one wall of clothes. "These are some really nice things," she said. "You sure there's no one you know who wants them?"

He shook his head. "Emily and I…kind of lost touch with our friends after the accident. People cared, they stopped by, but it wasn't like we could do much. And after she died…a couple of her closest friends offered to help me clear out her stuff, but… I didn't want them around. I know that sounds awful, but their pity…and their grief… I didn't want the first and didn't know how to handle the second."

It seemed so long ago now. A different lifetime.

"Is there anything here that you want to keep? Anything that means something special to you?"

It all meant something special. Even the shirts he couldn't really even remember her wearing. He'd saved a few items, all of the good jewelry, her wedding dress, in case he had a girl who would want it. Or a son whose wife might. Maybe even a granddaughter someday…

"Please, take it all. It would make me feel good to know that other women are taking pleasure from it," he told her. "I know it would make Emily happy. The shoes, belts, costume jewelry, anything you think they'd appreciate and use." He grabbed a box. Started taping one end.

He wanted it gone.

He had their baby on the way. Would always love and honor her as the mother in their little family. And as his best friend and soul mate.

But the daily living, with Emily first in his thoughts—that was done.

He was letting go.

On Friday of that week, four weeks after implantation, Christine had another appointment with the fertility specialist. She'd be followed by both Dr. Adams and her ob-gyn until twelve weeks or so, when the former passed off all care to the latter. Until then, the two were consulting with each other.

Christine liked Dr. Adams quite well. She just wasn't as familiar with her and wasn't quite as relaxed as she'd liked to have been when her name was called. Jamie was going to get his first glimpse of his baby with an early ultrasound—something Dr. Adams always did at four weeks after implantation—and Christine had purposely chosen the primary colored flowered skirt and short-sleeved yellow cotton top on purpose because of the elastic waistband and ease of raising the shirt. And maybe, just maybe she'd chosen the outfit because Jamie was going to be there and she felt like she looked good in it. She hoped not, but couldn't deny that she'd wanted to feel good about herself.

And he'd be the most likely reason. The ultrasound technician sure wasn't going to care.

Jamie, who looked too—everything—in his tan pants and black short-sleeved shirt, stood as soon as she did.

He walked just behind her as she followed the technician down the hall and into a fairly large shadowed room. This was it.

Visual proof that there was actually a little body forming inside her. Hopefully confirmation that, so far at least, it was growing as expected. Was healthy.

And then came that moment when she had to get up on a table and have her belly bared down to her pubic hair while Jamie was watching.

Not the way she'd like to be getting partially naked with the man. Or have him see her naked.

But the only way that it was ever going to happen.

She wanted to be relieved about that.

Jamie's first glance of Christine's belly exposed on the examining table might have been a bit of a struggle for him to get through, except that he couldn't really see her. Not her belly. If he leaned slightly, he could see her face. The technician, Danielle she'd said her name was, had positioned him in the best place to see the monitor, and it happened to be right behind her, the technician, who mostly blocked his view of Christine.

She talked to them about the coolness of the gel, about the process, and then said, "Let's see what we've got," in an almost singsong voice.

Heart pounding, he stared at the screen. Hard. Saw shadows, some much lighter than others. He'd seen sonograms on television, had seen one that friends of his and Emily's had shown around a few years before when they'd been expecting their first child.

He'd looked at some pictures during his reading over the past few months.

But this wasn't like any of that. The screen in front of him—that wasn't just a picture. It was his life. More valuable than his life, though.

"Here we are," Danielle said, seeming to direct her words over her shoulder to Jamie, not to Christine who, other than saying she was fine, hadn't spoken a word. He glanced at her face. She was lying there with her eyes closed.

Not looking at the screen.

Not sharing the moment.

"This is your baby," Danielle said, pointing to the screen. He could barely make out the form that outlined the baby, but he got there. Stared. Could hardly believe it.

When he looked closely, he could actually make out a head. A torso. The beginnings of a human being. And it hit him so hard he lost the air from his lungs.

He was going to be a father.

A real, flesh and blood father.

He glanced from the screen to Christine, needing her to know how much her gift meant to him. He'd never be able to thank her enough. To repay her.

Her eyes were still closed, but he thought he saw a tear slide down the side of her cheek. He could have been wrong. The room was illuminated only by under cabinet lighting above the counter along one wall. He hoped he was wrong.

The last thing he wanted was for his future joy to be causing her pain.

Clearly Danielle had been told that the baby wasn't Christine's. That she was only the surrogate. The woman had been completely respectful and attentive to Christine's physical comfort, but she'd placed the monitor so that Jamie could see it clearly. Christine would have had to turn her head over and up to see.

She discreetly thanked the technician as they left the room less than ten minutes from the time they'd entered. Jamie already had a strip of printed photos in hand. She could see them if she looked.

She didn't.

She'd prepared herself to feel the baby kick inside her. To care about it and then, as soon as it left her body, to move on down the road.

For some ungodly reason, she'd failed to think about how watching the miracle of its growth would affect her. She'd only had one ultrasound with Ryder.

She'd stared at that photo for hours, slept with it under her pillow, carried it in her purse, all those weeks she'd thought she would be keeping her baby.

And when she'd made the difficult decision to give him up, she'd put the photo away, upstairs in a trunk in the attic, and had never looked at it again.

"Right in here," Danielle said, leading them to an opened door leading into an office with a big messy desk and two chairs directly in front of it, telling them to have a seat.

She didn't want to have a seat. Not in the enclosed space, alone with Jamie. She just needed a minute or two by herself. To breathe and distract her mind from things she couldn't change and guide it to that which made her happy. Her work. The clients at The Parent Portal. The lives of the healthy children she'd helped others bring into the world. The families her work helped create. Picturing the bulletin board filled with their pictures on a sidewall in her home office, she took the seat closest to the door.

And talked about the fact that it looked like it was going to rain. There was a window in the room. She focused on the sky and tree limbs she could see beyond it.

Dr. Adams didn't keep them long. She didn't have a lot to say, other than that everything looked pretty good. She was a little concerned about the lining of Christine's uterus, wasn't sure it was thickening as much as she'd like. Said she wanted them back for another ultrasound in a month and said that while there was absolutely no worry, she might put Christine on progesterone shots as the pregnancy progressed.

"I don't understand," Christine said, sitting up straight. "I had no problems whatsoever when I carried my son. I'm older now, but still well within healthy childbearing years…"

She was making too much of a small thing. She knew it even as she said the words. This whole thing was hard enough, though, without finding out that there was something lacking in her.

Dr. Adams smiled, shaking her head. "If you'd conceived naturally I suspect there'd be no issue," she said. "And there might not be one at all. If this were a natural conception, I wouldn't even be concerned. But we see this sometimes when we're dealing with implantation. The surrogate's body doesn't produce the hormone quite as profusely as it might normally do. It's just something we watch."

She nodded. Feeling like she was going to cry anyway. She'd never even considered the fact that she might not be good enough to get this job done. This was what she had to give. She'd damn well get it right.

"The progesterone has no negative effect on the fetus," Dr. Adams explained, "although in rare cases, if the baby's a boy, he could have one of the most common birth defects we see. It has to do with his urethra placement, but even if that were to happen, it's generally easily treated with no adverse effects."

"And the side effects for Christine?"

"The injections themselves can be painful. There might be discomfort at the site. But otherwise there are no negative effects."

"And if she needed the injections and didn't have them?" Jamie asked.

Christine felt his glance on her, but couldn't look at him. She really just wanted to get out of there. Get herself together. Hit some balls against the wall until she was her normal self.

"Then you risk her losing the baby."

"Well, that's not going to happen," she said. "Not if I can help it."

She nodded. She'd already been given progesterone before the implantation. "So, are we done here?" she asked, looking from the doctor to Jamie. "Or, at least, done with me?"

The doctor nodded. Jamie stood.

And Christine got the hell out of there.

Chapter Fourteen

Jamie wasn't all that surprised when he walked out into an empty waiting room. Christine wasn't in the parking lot, either. Nor was her car.

Disappointment settled around his edges at a time when he should be flying to the moon. Or, at least, be fully focused on the family he was making. Feeling a bit bittersweet was understandable, probably even healthy, considering that his wife wasn't there physically to share the experience with him.

Feeling let down because his surrogate wasn't sharing the moment could not be healthy. He needed her to have her own life. Because he expected her to deliver the baby and hand it to him.

She'd been right to leave.

The reminder of who and what they were to one another had been a kindness.

He went to Mission Viejo, sat in his office on campus and met with a few students, individually, who were in town prior to classes starting and needed to discuss their academic futures with him. Thought about calling his mother and letting her know she was going to be a grandma, but wanted to wait until they'd surpassed the three-month mark. Between one in four and one in ten natural pregnancies, or 10 to 25 percent, resulted in miscarriage. And more than 80 percent of the lost pregnancies occurred within the first twelve weeks. Some authorities said those risks increased with implantation.

He'd done his reading.

And needed the stats to back up the material. He made sense of his world through numbers.

And, perhaps, numbers failed to consider key factors that could leave him with less than expected.

The thought shot through him as he was on the freeway home to Marie Cove. Emily had often teased him, laughed with him, about the spaces she filled up for him. Like their first dance at their wedding. He hadn't given a single thought to a song he'd like for that dance. It just hadn't factored in to his thoughts concerning that day.

He'd wanted to be married and be done.

He had wanted to celebrate. The wedding just hadn't seemed like some humongous, life-changing moment to him but rather a continuation of a life that they'd already been living, another milestone on the road they'd been traveling since they were kids.

And then there was the time he'd been in a car accident and hadn't called her right away. His vehicle was totaled, but he and everyone else involved, including the young kid at fault, were fine. She hadn't laughed about that one. She'd been truly upset with him, telling him his calm was a wonderful asset most times, but there were moments that required more. She hadn't been able to fill the gap in his emotional maturity for him that time. She'd fallen into it.

So was Christine Elliott doing the same? Had he pushed this whole baby thing, certain of his "life" calculations, without considering key factors? The things you couldn't measure?

Like love? Sacrifice? Pain?

He'd asked a woman who spent her life caring for others and helping them have the families they wanted, to grow and protect his child, without considering the emotional ramifications to her. Not that she couldn't take care of herself, but he should have taken Christine's well-being into account…

And he hadn't given nearly enough weight to the physical impact it would have on her. The energy it would take to carry around all the extra weight every second of every day. Weekly injections that would not only be uncomfortable to receive, but left discomfort in their trails. The birth.

Why those possible shots brought it all home to him, he didn't know. Maybe it was the reality of having seen the baby inside of her. The concrete proof that there was more than just a flat stomach going on in Christine's midsection.

The almost panicked way she'd left the doctor's office…

As soon as he was back in town, he went straight to her office. Told she was at the racquetball court, he drove there.

He texted her. Let her know he was outside. Would have left immediately if she'd asked him to do so. When she sent back You up for a game instead, he quickly grabbed his bag out of the back of his vehicle and headed inside to the locker room.

The silver shorts and black T-shirt were clean. He changed out the contents of the bag every night—part of his bedtime ritual. He was at the door to her court in five. Planning to go easy on her—and his baby—he hoped to find a way to apologize for his lack of more thorough emotional forethought where their situation was concerned. And to talk to her about the injections.

Just because he took things calmly didn't mean others were capable of the same. It had taken Emily a long time to help him see that one can't choose which emotions to feel.

How one deals with those emotions is their choice.

The first sight of Christine in black spandex shorts

and a purple, close-fitting T-shirt sent a slew of feelings raging right down to his crotch.

He knew what to do with them. Wasn't sure telling them to be gone was enough. Ignoring them helped. Nothing really worked.

He still wanted her.

"You serve," she said, tossing him the little rubber ball and grabbing an extra paddle out of a bright yellow duffel bag in the back corner.

He did. Lightly. Barely giving effort to his movement.

And was promptly scored upon.

So noted. He'd give his attempt a bit more oomph. Racquetball required finesse. And physical effort. But not the strength he used to serve an ace out on the tennis court.

By the fourth serve, he was using every bit of strength he used when he was playing to win on the tennis court. Neither of them had said a word, other than to announce score. Christine didn't run all over the room. For the most part, she hardly moved, other than with her upper body. She just commanded the room from where she stood. Knew exactly how and where to place the ball, with how much punch, in order to make it hardest for him to return.

She didn't move, but she had him running all over.

By the second game, he'd caught on. Paid attention to strategy. Power. Placement. He still lost, but this game was a lot closer.

And then, when he was gearing up for the best three out of five, she stopped. "That's it for me," she said. "I'm giving myself an easy hour or a hard half hour," she said. "I'm not going to overdo it." Hardly sweating, she approached him, took his racquet and grinned at him. "I'm pregnant, you know."

His penis hardened at the sight of that grin. Thank God for loose T-shirts. And the support of boxer briefs.

As her gaze met his, he grew serious. "I wanted to see you, to let you know, seriously, that I don't just expect you to do the injections as a precaution. Obviously, if the baby's life is seriously at risk, I'll ask for them, but your comfort, both emotionally and physically, are equally important, Christine. You're a person, not a machine. You matter, and your well-being counts as much as anyone's."

He'd repeated the words in his brain all the way home from the university. By the time he'd given them voice, they sounded rehearsed. Not sincere.

The whole point in seeing her, rather than calling, was so that she could see how much he meant what he said.

"It's all in the contract, Jamie," she told him, sandwiching his racquet together with hers and putting them, and the ball, in her bag—her backside in full view as she bent over.

Wrong of him to notice. He cleared his throat. Turned a bit. "I'm not talking about the contract," he said. "I'm talking about two people, you and me. And I'm telling you, I'm not going to hold you to sentences in a contract that give me the right to decide matters like these—choices that don't affect your health, but could affect the baby's. The injections won't affect your health, according to Dr. Adams, but they'll affect your physical comfort. I'm telling you that we will consider together whether or not you do them."

Turning, her bag strap on her shoulder, with one foot propped up behind her, she leaned against the wall. Her short dark hair was mussed, looked windblown and far too sexy.

It also made him want to wrap his arms around her and protect her from anything in the world that might cause her pain.

Like what—he was some he-man of old and she was a damsel in distress? The idea almost made him laugh inside. He'd never been one of those guys that had to prove their masculinity by thinking there were others who were weaker than him. And Christine would never resemble a damsel in distress. Or any other kind of person who couldn't take care of herself just fine.

"I appreciate your consideration," she said, after watching him for a moment. "It's nice," she said. "Really nice. And noted."

He heard a "but" coming and waited for it.

"If something comes up that becomes an issue,

then I hope you'll still feel the same," she said. "But the injections won't be an issue, either way," she told him, her expression easy. Calm. "If I need them, I'll do them. It's not a big deal."

Painful injections on, at minimum, a weekly basis? Okay, so it wasn't peeling off skin or anything, but...

"They won't be nearly as painful as giving birth," she told him, with a cock of her head. Reminding him that she knew what she was talking about.

He'd never witnessed a birth live. She'd done more than that.

"It'll be an extra minute out of my day once a week," she said.

She'd been so upset in Dr. Adams's office that morning. But it apparently hadn't been about the injections. Maybe he'd known that from the beginning. Maybe he just wasn't sure how to talk about the emotional pain being pregnant seemed to have been causing her that morning.

Maybe he'd been wrong about that tear he'd seen.

And her abrupt departure from their appointment?

"More than a minute. You'll need to make weekly trips to the doctor's office and..."

She was shaking her head.

"Progesterone shots can be given in the thigh. I can do that myself."

He shook his head. Sure, some diabetics and others learned how to give themselves injections, but it took time. He'd watched his father's struggle when he'd had to do at-home injections. He knew this one. "You'd have to learn how to…"

Her headshake back interrupted him. "Enough already, Jamie. I knew what I was doing when I signed the contract and I'm fine. I'm a pro at giving injections," she said. "I've been doing them since I was in junior high. My grandmother was diabetic," she said. "I spent all of my junior high and high school years coming home for lunch to give her her shots. She said Gramps hurt too much when he gave them and she had a needle paranoia and couldn't give them to herself. Her hands weren't really steady enough, either."

"You left school every day?" He stood there, wanting to stay and chat for as long as she'd allow it. "You never had lunch with your friends?"

Shrugging, she said, "I had great lunches. Gram was a phenomenal cook, and she always had something good waiting for me."

He wanted to say more about how she'd missed out on some of the most important teenage socialization time, but knew that no good would come from pointing that out. Realized, too, that she'd know more than he what she'd sacrificed. "Maybe that's why I don't remember you from high school," he said. "Emily and I looked you up in our junior and senior yearbooks, and neither of us recognized you."

"I was two years younger, not in any of your classes."

"And never in the cafeteria," he said, beginning to understand a bit more who Christine Elliott really was. A woman who'd been sacrificing herself seemingly most of her life, to tend to others.

He didn't like being one of those using her to find his own happiness.

Who tended to her beside Christine herself?

Who sacrificed for *her*?

Jamie didn't like questions without answers.

Problems without solutions.

But he sure as hell liked her.

Too much.

Chapter Fifteen

The next seven weeks settled into a routine that transitioned to a sense of normality. Christine lived her life as she had before impregnation: working, volunteering, spending a couple of evenings a week at the center, having dinner out with friends. Racquetball changed from focusing on rigor to precision. And her diet changed a bit, with the addition of vitamins and the omission of foods she used to like but suddenly had no taste for, plus those she could no longer eat. Tuna was first on her list of foods no longer welcome anywhere near her. The smell made her nauseous, exactly as it had the first time she'd had a baby—and that was the extent of any signs of morning sickness. Just like back then.

So many similarities. Right down to giving up the child at the end of the pregnancy. She'd done it before. She could do it again. And it should hurt less this time. The baby wasn't biologically hers; she knew it was going to a loving home. And she had the chance to see it if she wanted to.

Her clothes were getting a little tighter, and her stomach developing a paunch so slight most wouldn't even notice.

Olivia continued to be her dear heart. It was like the pregnancy was drawing them closer. The pediatrician was in clear support of her "project" but was focused on Christine's emotional well-being more than anything.

The biggest change in her life, though, was the few times a week she met up with Jamie Howe. They'd have a bagel downtown, meet up at a big box store if they both had shopping to do. A couple of times he filled her car at a gas station, saying that this was part of her living expenses. She'd argued, telling him that she was receiving a monthly stipend that covered those, but gave in when he agreed to only catch a few of the tanks full along the way, because of the extra driving she was doing to meet him.

He'd been to her house once, to interview a plumber with her because it was someone she didn't know, but whose bid had been the most economical, and with her pregnant he hadn't wanted her alone in the house with a stranger, but he'd left almost as soon as the plumber had. They'd agreed with a look and a mutual shake of the head that she wasn't going to hire the guy. Sometimes the lowest bid wouldn't be the cheapest way to get the job done in the long run.

The sale on his house had closed, but a week before he was to give up vacancy, thirty days after closing, the inspection on the home he was purchasing came back with possible foundation problems. His old home's new owners had made a deal to allow him to stay put, renting the house for two months, while possible repairs were completed. She'd been with him to meet the inspector at the new house only because they'd gone three days without seeing each other and that was the only time they both had free.

She'd taken the baby to see his or her new home. To hear Daddy's voice. Jamie didn't have to be speaking with her to make that happen. She only needed to be near.

Their arrangement could be considered a bit overkill. She got that. And yet, with current studies showing how much a baby could be affected by environment in utero, she wanted to give Jamie every chance to bond with his child.

They tended to do things where there was no chance for a lot of personal conversation, and instead they ended up discussing how their days had gone, how his math as a way of art design classes had overfilled and he'd agreed to open one more to take up the slack. They kept a professional boundary between them, separating them at all times.

And that was good.

When Jamie called the Sunday morning before their twelve-week ultrasound appointment the upcoming Friday, inviting her to lunch at the country club, Christine balked for the first time.

"You really think that's a good idea?" she asked him. "I mean, downtown, anywhere we're out and about, we're going to be seen together, but at the country club...that's your tribe. You'll know pretty much everyone and..."

It just seemed awkward to her.

"I spend a lot of time there, and we've never been. The baby's going to be growing up there. And...they have a phenomenal Sunday brunch. We used to go every week. It was like a thing. You'd see a lot of the same people. I've been avoiding it since Emily died and figured that now would be a good time to get back out there. In another week, I'm going to start telling people that I'm going to be a father," he said. "My employers. My associates. Friends. My mother and stepdad. It's not like I'm just going to start showing up in everyone's lives with a baby in tow, like it appeared in the night by immaculate conception."

She'd wondered how he was going to handle that. But...

"A lot of these people are going to hear through the grapevine, Christine. I'd like them to see that

I'm out, I'm fine. To have a heads-up, sort of, before they hear the news."

"I just…don't want people to think that you and I…that we…"

The thought of people seeing them together and thinking they were a couple… Assuming they were…

She and Jamie had been out and about for weeks. She'd never worried about what people thought. Those who knew her knew what she was doing.

So why did she suddenly think it mattered what people thought?

She didn't know what she was thinking. Just…the country club…the sense that everyone knew everyone…the gossip of powerful people…

The idea that what they'd think wasn't true and that she didn't want them to know it wasn't…

Because she *wanted* it to be true?

She gave her head a vigorous shake.

"How about if I introduce you as a business associate?" he asked. "Then people won't try to make us out to be more than we are."

Maybe. It could work.

But the country club…

She'd been there for business purposes before. In a group, not one-on-one. Those tables for two— they'd always seemed so romantic to her. People living a life she'd never have—not because of the cost, but because she wasn't going to be part of a couple.

It was a life she didn't want.

Those couples at those tables, they'd seemed so intimate. Letting themselves be seen out together in a room filled with their peers. Not just with patrons, but with people who knew them. Like they were making some kind of announcement.

She had no real reason to object. But felt pressure closing in on her. Because when she pictured herself with Jamie at the country club, she'd suddenly wanted to be there as herself.

Not as the body carrying his child.

And that was all wrong.

As it turned out, it wasn't just her and Jamie out for lunch, and they weren't at a table for two. Christine chided herself as she sat down at a table for five and was introduced to Tom, Judge Tom Sanders; his lawyer and close friend, Michael Waterson; and Jamie's lawyer, Tanya Brennan. In her brightly colored floral sundress and red sandals, she felt a bit foolish for the extra attention she'd given to makeup and matching jewelry, thinking that she was going to be on display at a table for two.

"I hope you don't mind joining the others," Jamie had said quietly to her as he'd walked her toward them from the parking lot where he'd been waiting for her. It wasn't like she was a member of the club and could walk right in like the rest of them. She could be if she wanted to be. She could use her mother's inheritance for her own aggrandizement. She just didn't want to. "Tanya and Michael work in the same firm and were having lunch with Tom. When he saw me in the parking lot, he was delighted I'd rejoined Sunday brunch and invited us to join them."

"It's fine," she said, had to say, really. Reminding herself that these get-togethers with Jamie were at his pleasure, part of the contract, allowing his baby to become familiar with sounds from the life he or she would be living. Part of why he was paying her such a hefty sum.

Yes, she had a say in the when and where. She didn't just have to show up wherever or whenever he told her to. But, she did have to agree to show up on a regular basis. His money guaranteed her cooperation.

She'd kind of lost sight of the funds along the way. Because, other than living expenses, she wasn't spending any of it until she'd passed the first trimester. She wasn't just being a good Samaritan, helping him out. She'd been hired to do a job.

And that job didn't entail noticing how delicious he looked in long, very nicely fitting tan pants and a brown polo shirt that hugged his biceps. Nor did it entail the peek at his butt when he moved in front of her to greet the people at the table. She hadn't meant to do that. He'd just leaned right when she'd been assessing seating arrangements and there he'd been. In her line of vision.

It didn't take her long to figure out that Judge Sanders's personal lawyer, Michael, and he had lunch often. While it wasn't clear to Christine why Tanya, Jamie's surrogacy attorney, was having lunch with the judge and Michael, she figured it wasn't her business.

Until, five minutes after they'd all made polite introductions and ordered beverages to accompany the three-room, sumptuous brunch buffet, Judge Sanders, instead of heading toward the food as their waitress had suggested, looked across at Jamie and Christine, who were sitting side by side—with Michael next to Jamie and Tanya next to Christine.

"I asked Michael to do some research for me, and he sought Tanya's expertise as well," he said, somehow looking as powerful as if he'd been in a robe and up on his bench, even in a light green polo shirt and white pants. "They're about to tell me what they found out, and I figured, since you two are here, you might as well hear it as well." He glanced from her to Jamie. "That way if we have any action to take, we can be in agreement on what it should be."

She didn't want lunch. Or the juice she'd just ordered. "Do I need my lawyer here?" she asked, glancing at Tanya and Michael, too.

"Not at this point," Tanya said. "May I?" She looked to Michael, who nodded and then at the judge, who also gave his okay with a lift of his hand.

"The judge was concerned about his rights to the

baby, in the event that something ever happens to Dr. Howe," she said, smiling toward Jamie.

He smiled back. Not a sexy smile. A polite one. And she was reminded that they knew each other. That they'd worked together on the contract that bound him to Christine. Them against her, if there was ever a legal battle between them. A need to enforce the contract.

Shards of jealousy shot through her, shocking her. Christine didn't *get* jealous. Found the emotion a complete waste of time. Counterproductive to… productivity.

"Isn't it a conflict of interest for you to be advising the judge and Dr. Howe at the same time?" she asked. Because she was feeling stupidly defensive.

Stupidly wanting to put some kind of distance between Jamie and this…this…perfect woman. His professional equal. Which could matter a lot to him, being a college professor and holding a doctorate like he did. Her little master's degree in health management suddenly seemed less significant.

Which was ludicrous. She knew it even as she acknowledged the strong and completely unfamiliar negative emotions passing through her.

What in the hell was wrong with her?

The only answer that made any sense was hormones.

The seconds it took her to come up with an explanation she could live with had her missing the first bit of Tanya's reply.

She checked back in at, "Since I'm not in any way representing the judge, just reporting what I know about this particular area of the law, and because Dr. Howe knew when he sought out our firm that we represent Judge Sanders, it's within my legal jurisdiction to have the conversation. I'm not in any way reporting any parts of Dr. Howe's agreements, contracts, or dealings with our firm to the judge. Only giving general information regarding the law."

Wow. The woman had that down. Christine nodded, feeling stupid for having asked the question. After all, they were sitting with a superior court judge. But as the surrogate, she knew she was within her rights to question legalities.

"The bottom line is that California law states that grandparents have the rights to visitation of their grandchildren if certain requirements have been met. One is that the grandparent would need to show that there is an existing bond between the child and the grandparent. It would be up to you, Dr. Howe, to provide Judge Sanders with that opportunity…"

"I included Tom in this process before I'd even consulted Christine," Jamie said, looking to Tom and between the lawyers. "Of course he's going to have a bond with my child."

Tanya nodded. "Again, I'm not here to advise on particular circumstances, just to give you generalities in terms of the law, and I'm trying to lay them out in as clear a way as possible so that there are no surprises."

She was covering her own backside, Christine thought. And was ashamed of herself. The other woman was doing her job. Well.

And with compassion.

Feeling surreal, sitting there in that situation without forewarning, Christine tried to rein in emotions gone haywire. To find her zen.

"Excuse me," the judge spoke up, glancing at Christine. "Please understand, I didn't foresee this meeting happening with you sitting here, though I'm glad that you are here so we can all be on the same page. I want you to know that I am immensely grateful to you for giving of yourself so unselfishly and making it possible for our family to grow." It was the first time he'd looked in her direction since he'd said a quick hello and briefly shaken her hand during introductions. "I'm also a lawyer, and a judge who's seen all kinds of things in my courtrooms over the years. But never surrogacy. I can read the law. I wanted to know current surrogacy case law..."

"You're fine," Christine said. "I'm just having lunch per my surrogacy contract." She could feel Jamie's eyes on her. Found a professional smile and pasted it on.

"Surely you don't think I'd ever deny you rights to

your grandchild," Jamie stated, his gaze compassionate, not angry, as it moved to his former father-in-law.

"Of course I don't," the judge said, patting Jamie's hand where it lay on the table. "You're as much a son to me as Emily was a daughter—you know that."

Already feeling like an interloper, Christine hadn't thought it could get any worse. But there it was, taking everything she had to stay seated at the table.

Even while knowing that no one had said anything designed to make her feel unwanted. Anything that should even have had that effect on her.

She'd thought she was coming out for lunch with Jamie. Just the two of them. Being the nebulous "them" they'd somehow become.

"The judge's concern had more to do with if something happens to Jamie," Michael said, repeating a key point from the beginning of the conversation. "Before the baby's born. Or afterward."

"Before it's born… I didn't even think of that," Jamie said, frowning as he glanced around the table. "I should have thought of that."

"You're talking about estate planning," Christine said, jumping into the conversation at the sound of his consternation. "A lot of people don't think about it until after they've had children. And even then, it's not the first thing they run out and do."

While, after research, she'd made the decision not to include estate planning counseling as part of

The Parent Portal, she had added the requirement of legal documents regarding embryo ownership in the event that a spouse died. That was why Jamie had been able to use Emily's embryos in the first place.

"I was planning to talk to you about it as soon as I gathered the necessary information," Judge Sanders said. "That's what this meeting is about. Finding out what we need to do to protect ourselves." He glanced at Christine again, assessed her, and with a frown, moved his glance toward Jamie. "I need to be certain that we're protected in case something happens to you before the baby's born. We need to know that in the event that that happens, the child stays in our family. With me. With your mother..."

She wasn't a lawyer. Or a doctor of any kind. But she got where this was going.

"You're afraid I'll try to keep it."

"There have been cases where the surrogate tries to keep the baby, yes," he said. "But with legal contracts in place beforehand, the baby will be protected from being a ward of the state while any lawsuits or custody battles are fought."

Thoughts flew through Christine's mind as the conversation continued around her. She had to take a step back. She was the professional here, not a member of the family. Not anyone personally involved.

She wasn't going to try to keep anyone's baby. She was the one who'd already given one away. They had no idea who they were dealing with.

And...if something happened to Jamie...their agreement that she got to have contact with the baby this time...would that change?

Jamie had asked Tanya if they needed a separate contract to determine estate matters in the event of his death. Michael was talking about a case he'd read about, something recently on the books having to do with an adopted child...

Not a surrogacy case. Not her concern.

How in the hell had she thought she could do this?

And why was she struggling so hard to do it? It wasn't like she'd considered, even for a second, that the baby inside her was hers. Or that she'd have any connection to it once she birthed it.

But she cared about it. Deeply. As would a nurse in a NICU, taking care of a patient. She'd remember this child for the rest of her life, think of it now and then, pray that it was doing well...

"So I can handle this through an estate attorney?" Jamie was asking. "I just need to name a guardian for the child in my will. And that will cover us in the event something happened to me before the baby's born and afterward as well."

"In conjunction with the surrogacy contract, that's correct." Michael answered that time as well.

Christine didn't know if she liked him or not. Mostly she just wanted to be done with the brunch obligation and on with her day.

If she didn't step foot in the country club again anytime soon, that would be fine, too.

No one seemed to be giving them curious glances, as she'd imagined they might, but she figured those who were curious would find other ways of sneaking peeks without being overt about it. They'd be sure to wonder why the judge and his former son-in-law were meeting with attorneys. And maybe wonder who Christine was.

She'd been leaning away from Jamie—not wanting them to think she was there specifically with him. It helped that he hadn't looked at her since the judge had spoken to her.

"Okay, good, let's go get some lunch," Judge Sanders said, standing while the others followed suit. Jamie turned to her; she saw him do it from the other side of the table. She'd scooted ahead of Tanya, to put herself between the two lawyers. She'd need to sit next to Jamie, to give the baby as much chance as possible to hear his voice. Maybe she should sit between the two men, so the baby could get familiar with both voices...

"Ms. Elliott?" Judge Sanders's booming voice called her to attention just as she was reaching for a plate—and noticed that the others had all moved on, taking plates from the identical stack of them across the room.

"Yes, sir?"

"I just… I'm sorry."

She smiled, just wanting to get away. "You have nothing to be sorry for," she said, picturing herself behind her desk, speaking with a client.

Any client but Jamie.

"I was harsh," he said, and the catch in his voice drew her attention. She glanced into his green eyes and saw pain there. "Harsher than I generally am. You're unselfishly giving us a great gift, and yet… I look at you and I feel resentment…"

His voice broke. And she understood. Hearing a replay of a conversation she'd had with Jamie many weeks before.

Nodding her head, she started to speak, but he said, "It's so hard…my Emily should be…" His voice broke and his eyes moistened.

"It's okay, Judge," she said, reaching out to touch his hand without questioning herself. "I truly do understand. This isn't an easy situation. It's going to have hard parts for all of us. I just hope that, in the end, it brings you and Jamie, and the little one, more joy than any of you could imagine."

Because that's what families did.

She knew. She'd had one once. With her mom and dad. And then again with her grandparents.

And had almost had another—before she'd given him up to a family that had a much better chance at bringing him more joy than struggle.

She just had to keep her mind on the prize—giving two very nice men a new family member. And in so doing, giving them a piece of their family back.

Chapter Sixteen

The twelve-week ultrasound went about the same as the first. Jamie couldn't see much but the screen and Christine's face. The technician had spoken mainly to him again. As far as he'd seen, Christine had kept her eyes closed. She'd left as soon as they met with Dr. Adams, though he'd known this time that she'd scheduled the appointment in between meetings at The Parent Portal.

Good news was that the fertility specialist was pleased with her uterine lining and Christine shouldn't need injections. Dr. Adams had turned over the remainder of the prenatal care to Dr. Miller, Christine's regular ob-gyn. The sonogram had been inconclusive regarding the sex of the child.

He hated that Christine hadn't been there to hear the report with him. It hadn't seemed right, her having left before he'd heard the results.

He suspected she'd done so on purpose.

And didn't blame her.

He hadn't been able to stop grinning, looking at the film of his little one's movement, and when the sound of the baby's heartbeat echoed through the room, he'd teared up as chills shot through him. How did you know that life was growing inside you and also be okay with having no claim to it?

No right to it?

He wished he'd been more aware of what he'd been asking when he'd come up with the surrogacy idea. It could be that he'd have asked anyway, but at least he could have been more sensitive.

Exactly what he'd do differently, he didn't know, but, seeing how loving Christine was, how nurturing, he knew he'd have tried to do something.

They continued their thrice-weekly meetings without change on into September. As busy as he was with the additional class, along with tennis practices and driving into the university in Mission Viejo a couple of times a week, those hours with Christine were the highlight of his life. Partially because she was carrying his baby.

And partially because… He hoped to God he was suffering from transference. But as time went on, he didn't think so. She drew him like a magnet, and he knew all about the molecular structure that defined many magnetic properties. Physics made more sense to him than emotional transference. And still didn't explain why this one woman called out to him.

So he let it go as best he could. Lived his life one day at a time. Enjoying the days with Christine in them more than the ones from which she was absent.

He'd passed on the house he'd wanted to buy, having seen that the structural damage was just too great to be a good investment. He had had to put most of his things in storage and move in to a little rental property while he looked for something else.

Other than the fact that he was aware he needed a place to put the nursery furniture he'd ordered, as well as the various other baby items he'd been buying—a stroller, a year's worth of disposable diapers, lotions and towels with hoods, car seat and… The list went on and on—he wasn't hating the rental. He'd found a little cottage right on a stretch of the private beach that made Marie Cove so desirable to many of Los Angeles' elite. It was only a mile from Christine's house, and he liked the vicinity.

Liked that she was close.

He'd have to get a bigger place eventually, but until the baby was two or three, they'd be okay there.

He'd spent Labor Day with Tom, and video chatted with his mom, who'd wanted him to fly up to Oregon. She'd been calling him at least twice a week, and texting almost daily since finding out he was going to be a father. That she was finally going to be a grandmother, and was already making plans to fly down and stay with him after the baby was born.

He was grateful for the love. And for the help.

He just needed space left in his life for...

Christine.

She and her friend Olivia had spent the holiday at the women's center. He didn't actually speak to her, but when he'd texted to wish her a happy Labor Day, she'd sent a picture of her and the pediatrician standing behind three grills filled with burgers and more coleslaw than he'd ever seen in one place. They'd both been wearing aprons, and the huge grins on their faces had brought a smile to his. He'd saved the photo in his gallery.

His first photo of her.

On the Friday after Labor Day he invited her to his little cottage. He wanted to talk to her privately. And not in a business setting. He told her so right up front, giving her the chance to refuse, and then had difficulty maintaining his calm when she didn't.

He'd never had trouble remaining calm. Not until Christine had come along.

Until the baby had.

He'd like to believe that his emotional upheaval was more in line with sympathy pregnancy than anything else. That he was on the normal, preparental roller coaster.

And there was some of that, to be sure. The highs

and excitement, mixed with worries and insecurities about being a parent. A single, male parent.

None of it made him jittery. Anxious. Or manically active.

Only thoughts of Christine did that. He'd never been jittery with Emily.

He didn't get it. He'd never so much as held Christine's hand.

And yet the second he opened his door to her that next afternoon, he reached for her hand, guiding her inside like she couldn't find the way herself. All two steps of it.

Realizing what he'd done, he pulled back almost immediately, but his hand knew the soft touch of her skin. And his mind was holding on. It wasn't going to let him forget.

"Wow," he said then, standing back to stare at her. "You look...great!" She wore capri pants with a tight, long, colorfully striped top and wedge shoes.

It was the first time he'd seen the shape of her stomach so clearly. "You're...showing..."

He stared. Knew he was staring. Couldn't stop.

Her chuckle only served to make the moment more potent. "You've seen the sonogram, Dad," she said.

Silence fell and as his gaze rose to hers, she instantly sobered, her deep brown eyes locking him to her.

He was the host, but she recovered first. "So, what

did you want to talk to me about?" she asked, looking beyond him to the L-shaped great room that encompassed living, kitchen and dining areas. A small hall led to two bedrooms with a rather large bathroom in between. A side door off the kitchen led to a two-and-a-half-car garage—which was one of the reasons he'd landed on the place. It had lots of space to store the boxes he'd wanted closer than his rented storage facility.

He wanted to show her the spare bedroom, currently consumed by his baby purchases. Wanted her to ooh and ahh over them. To want to see every single purchase. To touch and feel. To voice her opinions and suggestions.

He wanted to hear them.

And to get all gooey at the sight of the tiny little onesies he'd picked up in the university bookstore.

"Right," he said instead, moving toward the couch and love seat that was fine for his home, but consumed the cabin's much smaller space. "Have a seat."

He offered her something to drink, but she lifted the aluminum water bottle she'd brought in with her and politely declined. Settled onto the edge of a cushion at one end of the couch.

Not planning to stay long.

Getting back to business.

A place he didn't want her to go.

"I wanted to talk to you about the future," he

started, settling with some difficulty onto the love seat cushion closest to her. He needed to walk. To move.

A reaction only she seemed to instill in him.

"What about the future?" Her frown was softened by the smile he'd grown to dislike: the one with professional stiffness about it. Not something he'd noticed when he'd first been a client in her office, but one that he'd learned well in the months they'd been together.

Learned well and started to dislike it being directed at him. Vehemently.

"I'd like you to play a part in the baby's life." When he put it starkly like that, all alone out in the world, he stiffened inside. "It's kind of a reverse surrogate wanting to keep the baby thing." He tried to lighten the moment and heard the miserable fail.

She hadn't moved. Just watched him, that horrible smile on her face.

"It sounds bad," he said. "You're already sacrificing so much, putting parts of your life on hold, to give me my chance at a family, and here I am asking for more. I just…now that we're in this situation… I'm seeing what I was really asking of you…"

Yes, but that wasn't what this was about, either.

"…So much more than to hire your body for nine months.

"You deserve to get to know the child you're carrying. What I'm trying to do is establish your relationship with the baby, if you want one. One of your choosing."

She still said nothing. Just sat there. Smiling at him. He saw no tremble in her lips to indicate she cared, no change of expression that let him know she'd even heard.

"I'm not asking you to give any more of yourself," he said. "I'm not asking you to do anything for the child, to sacrifice any more. I know our contract states that you can request the chance to see the child at some point, if the need arises. But I'm saying, the door's open for you to have the child in your life on a regular basis, from birth. Not as the mother, necessarily. Not with legal custody rights. But…there."

There. He'd finally gotten it right.

Partially.

Her smile had faded.

"I've… I like you, Christine. I like having you in my life. I'd like to think we've become friends. And that we can remain friends…"

And that was the other part. He didn't want the birth of his child to mean that he'd lose her.

She was blinking regularly. Breathing.

"Say something…"

Pursing her lips, she rocked a little bit, forward and back, the movement almost imperceptible. But there. Was she nodding? Comforting herself?

"I…uh…" She cocked her head, smiled at him

again. Mostly professionally, accompanied by a more personal glint in her eyes.

"Ever since that brunch with Tom at the country club…" He'd apologized profusely after that god-awful hour. She'd brushed him off as though the meeting had been of no personal concern. Had said she understood where Tom was coming from and was fine.

He'd had no choice but to let it go. To try to believe her. But…

"Before that even… I've begun to realize how selfish I've been and… The Parent Portal is all about the human element in fertility choices. It's what sets your clinic apart. You've given your whole life to the cause, and I've managed to put you in a situation that takes your own humanity out of it…"

"It's okay, Jamie."

No it wasn't. "Please, Christine, don't go all Ms. Elliott on me. I'm not a client here."

"Technically, I'm your employee."

He shook his head. "You've become a friend. One that means more to me than I can even understand…"

"Don't." Shaking her head, she held up a hand. It was trembling. "This…this is what's not okay," she said. "This is what's hard. I have a role to fill, Jamie. A job to do. And a reputation to uphold. Not just for me, but for The Parent Portal. My employees. Our clients. And future clients. The future families we can help bring to life…"

"I know."

"What you're saying here…it's like tempting a dog with a pork chop bone when, after he takes it and enjoys the moment, it's going to splinter inside him and could kill him."

His offer was like a bone to a dog. That's what he heard. She coveted what he wanted to give her. Was licking her chops and…

"I'm being selfish again." His brain finally got to the point she'd been making. His offer only made things harder on her. Not easier. While attempting to be kind, he'd ended up being kind of cruel.

"You're being human, and very sweet." The way she smiled at him, her trembling lips only slightly tilted, changed his world. "And if we weren't under legal contract, if we weren't dealing with a situation that was conceived at The Parent Portal…"

The conversation seemed to have ended as she trailed off, and the room seemed to darken. To lose air. Jamie glanced out toward the ocean. Wondering how to extricate them both from the very awkward situation he'd created. How to hide his already-exposed vulnerability once again.

"If…after the baby is born…you still want to make your offer, offers—friendship and a relationship with the baby—I will at least be open to having the conversation." She stopped. Just kept watching him.

Thinking? Assessing? He withstood the scrutiny. Waited for what she'd bring next.

"It actually does help, knowing that the birth might not be the end. Knowing that there's possibility." Her hand cradled the slight bump in her belly.

And the lights came back on.

Chapter Seventeen

During their sixteen-week visit Cheryl offered Jamie the opportunity for another ultrasound, to determine the sex of the baby, but he declined after looking at Christine.

"I don't mind," she'd told him, while they were still sitting in the doctor's office. "Truly, it's not a big deal." Not physically. And the rest... She was a pro. If there was any momentary residual emotional discomfort, she'd quickly get over it.

Besides, he'd offered her the chance to actually know the baby she was creating. He might change his mind. She wasn't the mother and had no legal rights. But the idea dangling out there made the pregnancy easier.

Not for any logical reason. It wasn't like she'd be a mother this time around. The child wouldn't know her as such. That would be too confusing. And unfair to all of them. But to actually be able to see the child, to see for herself that it was well, happy, thriving…

She brought up the ultrasound possibility again a couple of days after their Wednesday doctor visit, five days after he'd made his sweet offer in his cottage. They'd been for a walk on the private stretch of beach attached to his cottage—and several others along the way—and were sitting, in jeans and long-sleeved shirts, in the sand, about halfway between the ocean and the cottage. The Friday late afternoon air held a chill that was more invigorating than cold.

She was meeting Olivia for dinner at seven. Had to get home and change, but had been struggling to find a way to talk to him about things she really wanted to discuss, without compromising that professional glass wall standing between them.

Having asked if they could sit a moment, she suddenly felt like she'd created a hot seat for herself.

The ocean was rough, roaring into the beach in waves strong enough to knock over sandcastles and sweep them away. She and her father had made an entire colony out of sand once—huts and a store and a school with little twig benches…

"I want to order the ultrasound," she told Jamie. "I won't do it without your say-so, as you have to foot the bill since it's not required prenatal care at this point, but you wanted to know the sex of the baby the last time, and now they can tell."

He was shaking his head before she'd even finished. "I can wait."

"Jamie…" She turned her head, waited for him to look at her. Hadn't realized how close they were. Their shoulders weren't even touching, but his face was so close. A lean and a scoot and her lips could touch his. Could talk in a whole new way.

"You think I don't know it's hard on you to lie there and hear that heartbeat and divorce yourself from what's going on inside you?" he asked. "I've done more reading…the hormones that protect the baby affect you, too. There's natural bonding going on between you and the baby… I'm not going to put you through any more than absolutely necessary."

"You need to quit thinking about me, and let yourself get everything you can out of this," she said, a passion in her tone that surprised her. And seemed to knock him a bit off course as well. Wide-eyed, he glanced at her and kept looking.

"I signed on for this," she told him. "I've been pregnant before. I knew what I was letting myself in for. The nine months will be over and I'll go on with my life. But you…you're missing out, Jamie, by not letting yourself revel in it. Or celebrate it."

"How do you know I don't? You're only with me for short periods at a time a few times a week. That leaves a lot of celebration time."

He was right. She didn't know. The idea didn't sit well. Had she been so certain she really knew him? That she knew what he did with the majority of his life?

Confused, she forced her mind back on track.

"You're dying to know if you're having a boy or girl." She couldn't be wrong about that. She'd listened to the things he didn't say.

And the little things he had, like the time he'd mentioned a future with dance classes or fishing poles… It wasn't like he'd had a preference for one or the other, or even a need to have fishing poles if it was a boy; he'd just seemed to need to know. Because he was a guy whose numbers had to be concrete. Had to fit neatly within their formulas.

He was taking on solo a job for two. Not just a job. A lifetime commitment. With no professional boundaries.

He hadn't denied her statement.

"I'm scheduling the ultrasound," she said, standing.

He stood, too, and their hands brushed. Just briefly, they both froze. Looked into each other's eyes.

And she was glad she was pregnant with his child.

Jamie wasn't a reveler. His celebrations tended to be of the quieter kind. A sense of rightness inside him. Well-being.

But that next Friday, when he stood just behind a new technician, Molly, in a different ultrasound room located within Cheryl Miller's private practice clinic, and heard the words, "It's a boy!" he whooped right out loud.

He'd kind of been hoping for a girl who'd take after Emily. But there wasn't even a hint of disappointment in him as Molly pointed out the evidence.

"I'm going to have a son!" He couldn't believe the near squeal came from him, and instinctively, his gaze went to Christine. To share the miracle with her.

Her eyes were closed. There was no mistaking the couple of tear drops coming from their corners.

But she was smiling.

Christine had said he needed to celebrate, and he wanted to. But only with her.

The fact brought him up short as he drove away from the clinic that morning and headed straight to the public beach he'd shared with Emily all those years. To commune with his wife and sit with their baby news with her in the only way left to him.

Walking down as close to the shore as he could get without waves washing up on him, he plopped down in the dark brown dress pants and beige sweater he'd worn to class, and looked out to sea. To Emily.

The horizon met him with a blank stare. He looked for her face and saw Christine, eyes closed, with tears and a smile. Saw her on the private beach outside his cottage, looking at him like she needed to kiss him as badly as he needed to kiss her. And in her office the day he'd first made his request of her to carry his baby. Remembered her telling him that she was certain his request would be on her mind for years to come.

"We're having a son, Em!" He said the words aloud, releasing emotion that had been clamoring inside him.

He listened for Emily's response in his head, her excitement, and instead heard Christine's voice thick with emotion as she told him that he was offering pork to a dog.

What kind of an ass was he that a woman he'd only known for months was able to drown out the memory of the wife, the woman, the girl he'd loved for more than half his life?

What kind of a fool?

As the baby grew inside her, Christine worked longer hours at The Parent Portal and volunteered more. She was doing the healthy thing—keeping herself occupied with pursuits that brought value to her life. She took care of herself. Rested on the couch in her office at least a few minutes every morning and afternoon. Was eating like a health nut, down to measuring and weighing when she was at home to ensure that she got recommended amounts of all the nutrients that would help the baby boy to grow, and none that could hinder his growth.

Her body was his temple for the next few months, and when he returned it to her, he'd be leaving it in better condition, healthwise, than he'd found it. She'd have a few pounds to lose, some baby fat, but her cholesterol levels would be stellar.

At four and a half months pregnant, she'd gained seven pounds. Was aiming for a pound a week for the rest of the pregnancy. The last ultrasound hadn't been necessary but she'd been glad to have the confirmation that all was well. The baby's growth was right in the middle of the normal chart. Her uterine lining was nice and thick and protecting him. Her blood pressure was great, his heartbeat strong and steady.

She was having another boy. Very similar to something she'd already been through. Jamie's baby should have been the only thing different in her life. Her only focus. But how did you control your subconscious? She was waking up nights with Jamie Howe on her mind, as though he was in her bed with her, but when she opened her eyes, she lay there alone. Sometimes she remembered dreams. Sometimes she didn't.

It was all very confusing.

As was sitting in the most luxurious SUV she'd ever been in. But that Wednesday evening, he'd invited her to a musical being put on at the university in Mission Viejo. A couple of his students were working sound, another was a dancer, and Jamie was friends with the choral director—a man almost as old as Tom Sanders.

They'd eaten in the car on the way in—the dinner she'd packed was all healthy finger foods—because she'd had a late-afternoon appointment already scheduled.

Jamie didn't say a lot about the cucumber sandwiches and avocado deviled eggs, but he ate them until they were gone so she took that as a win. He talked almost the whole way—filling her in a little bit on each of his students who were involved because she might meet them. And talking about Daniel, the choral director's, operatic singing career. As they were parking, he let her know that Daniel knew about the baby, as did the college president who employed him.

He'd failed to tell his students, apparently, or hadn't found doing so appropriate, and she'd felt their eyes boring into her belly as they'd come in a group of three to say hi to Jamie in the vestibule after the show.

She'd just been getting used to the idea of accepting that strangers would naturally assume they were a couple and that the baby she was carrying belonged to both of them, not minding that they thought that, when he'd introduced her as his surrogate, and explained that she was carrying his and Emily's baby.

Apparently they'd been in his life long enough

to know about his deceased wife. As they were all three seniors, it made sense.

And after the play, her good mood slowly dissipated. For a bit there, she'd forgotten that she was only at the university so that the baby inside her could be exposed to the sounds. She'd forgotten she was working. She'd simply enjoyed the show, being with Jamie, hearing him laugh out loud.

She'd been in Mission Viejo so his baby could hear him laugh out loud.

Jamie kept up a string of conversation all the way home, too. Mostly about the play—an original, nonholiday tale about scientists and animals that was the culmination of a semester's work. He'd told her about sound levels and how his students used mathematical skills in their artistic creations in Mission Viejo as well. And how the dancer, who had sprained an ankle a month before, had been afraid she wouldn't be able to perform. There'd been more. She let it roll over her, hoping the baby inside her was paying attention to his voice.

And then she was waking up in her driveway, feeling as comfortable as if she'd been in her own bed.

"I'm so sorry! I didn't mean to drop off on you," she said. "I've been doing that lately...falling asleep anytime I'm sitting doing nothing."

"So, what, it's happened once?" he teased her.

His smile was illuminated by the streetlight in front of her house. She was as focused on the warmth those lips sent through her as she was on the fact that he'd turned off his SUV.

"I have something to talk to you about," he said, staying on his side of the vehicle, looking straight ahead, though the way he said the words sounded really personal.

Her heart started to pound as anticipation thrummed through her. Inappropriate anticipation.

"If this is more about the future... I meant what I said, Jamie. We can't..."

He was shaking his head.

"It's about now," he said. "I'd like permission to touch your stomach," he told her. "I was reading about the fact that mothers can feel their babies from the outside as well as inside, and that babies sometimes move to the touch."

She should have offered. She knew this stuff.

"Of course you can feel it, Jamie!" Loosening her seat belt, she let it slide back into its holster. "I'm sorry I made you ask." Pushing up the console between them, she moved over slightly and offered him access to her protruding belly, covered by the dress yoga pants and black, red, yellow, blue and white floral, formfitting tunic she'd put on because she'd thought they were festive.

Offering a new daddy the chance to bond with his baby.

She was not—absolutely not—wanting the feel of

Jamie's warm hand spread across her stomach. And if she was, then she would make the wanting stop.

She had to make it stop.

Because when those fingers lightly brushed against her top and then settled with confidence on top of her belly, her entire lower body melted.

Chapter Eighteen

She wasn't huge yet, but he'd been able to reach her baby bump easily.

From there, Jamie just froze. He'd read that if he moved his fingers, applied a very slight pressure, he might be able to distinguish parts of the baby. And might also be able to convince him to move. Chances of that were better as the pregnancy progressed.

He was struggling to separate Christine's stomach from the baby inside her. He'd feared his reaction from the moment he'd known he needed to bond with his son in this way. He trusted his ability to be a great father.

What he didn't trust was his libido. Not where this woman was concerned.

How did a guy feel his baby in a woman's stomach and want to have sex?

How could he feel his baby in a woman's stomach and not want to have sex?

As his body reacted to the feel of her beneath his palm in the quiet darkness of his car, he slowed his mind. Closed his eyes.

And knew that he'd never separate Christine from his son. She was helping to create him.

In the darkness behind his lids he couldn't hide from another truth. He was falling in love with the woman. Had already fallen in love with her.

It wasn't transference. It wasn't gratitude.

It was her.

Igniting things in him he'd never felt before. Not ever.

Not even with Emily.

What he did with any of it, other than calculate and catalog, he had no idea.

Moving his hand slightly to the left, he tried to make out a shape and... He jumped, pulling his hand off of Christine and then immediately putting it back down.

"What was that?"

"He just moved..." Her words ended on a lilt—a sound from her that was unfamiliar to him. "How cliché is that?" He heard clearly forced levity in her tone, and then, "It's like he knows you, Jamie. I've felt bubbles over the past week or two, but this is the first time I could really feel him move. And he did it for you…"

Her face was turned to his in the streetlight, her eyes glistening.

"He did it for both of us." The words slipped out in a reverent moment.

"No." Her tone had changed. Hardened, but not in a mean way. Just firm. She placed her hand over his, holding his hand in place when he might have lifted it. "He's doing this for you, Jamie."

She couldn't possibly know that. And most likely wasn't right, considering that the baby had no idea that the woman carrying him, protecting and caring for him, hadn't contributed an egg. Maybe the warmth of his bigger hand was a contributing factor, but…

He felt the tear drop on the side of his hand, a bare portion not covered by her smaller hand. She didn't pull away, or push him away, just sat there silently.

"We're human beings," he said softly, the words pouring up from a new source within him. "I can't possibly sit here and experience the first touch of my baby all alone. You're a part of it. Just as you can't sit there and endure whatever it is that hurts you and have me unaware."

Her hand slid off from his.

He continued to cradle her stomach.

"Let me share it with you, Chris."

"Only my mom and dad and Gram and Gramps call me that."

The news wasn't surprising. Only family was allowed to occupy the inner circle of her heart. Using her full name was a shield by which she kept the world from getting too close.

He'd grown to know her over the past months, in all of their innocuous conversation.

Their refusal to allow anything physical between them had left open another avenue of intimacy.

An emotional, mental recognition that he couldn't prevent.

"Let me share it with you, Chris," he repeated, not able to allow himself to be deflected from that goal. If she told him to go, he would do so. But if she let him stay, he was doing so as a friend. A man who cared about her.

Not as the father of the child she was carrying.

"I wanted to keep my first son."

What in the hell was she doing?

Reaching for the door handle, Christine held on to it. Ready to get out. The hand on her stomach compelled her to stay.

She was there to help Jamie bond with his baby, and he was doing so in the most incredible way. There was no mistake that the fetus had chosen right then to kick for the first time. To reach up from the womb that was giving it sustenance for the moment to the hand that would feed it for a lifetime.

She would not make the moment about her. Had to focus on him. On the goal at hand…

"Did you tell anyone?" His voice, soft in the darkness, oozed over her like warm chocolate. Soothing. Sweet. A reminder of happier times.

Of childhood.

She'd been such a happy kid.

Which made the sadness that had followed seem so much more acute.

"Yeah," she said. "My dad and his wife knew. I had my grandparents to consider, though. By my senior year they were both failing. If I wasn't there, helping them, they'd have had to sell the family home and move into assisted living. I couldn't do that to them. Not because I'd made a mistake. I couldn't abandon them, or force them to live out the end of their lives in what would have been, to them, a prison, not after they'd spent their lives taking care of all of us. Taking care of me. They were both mentally sharp. I went to my dad for help, trying to figure out a way to make it all work."

She'd already told him and Emily a bit about Ryder. Telling him a few more details didn't need to change anything in their relationship.

Except it did. She was letting him see her, the person. The woman who grieved, every single day, for the child she'd birthed and given up. And in his seeing, she had to see, too. Had to see how devastating it had been for her to let them take Ryder. And how incredibly painful she was finding the idea of knowing that when she gave birth to Jamie's child, she'd be losing that baby, too. Even as she justified herself, she rejected the justification. Knew she needed to just shut up.

The baby moved again. Not as energetically, but still completely decipherable, sending muscle memory waves through her entire body.

Resurrecting a memory so vivid it took her breath. And all of her focus. She was there again, lying in her bed, curled in a fetal position, cradling her belly with her hands, promising herself that she wouldn't give up her baby. Her father was taking her the next day to sign the adoption papers, and even while she sobbed and told herself she wouldn't do it, she knew she had to.

Because she loved her baby, and her grandparents, that much.

"Just because a person is old doesn't mean their life is less valuable," she said aloud. "I was in a position to tend to my grandparents. If they were in a home, I'd have no home. No way to provide for a baby. At least not in a way that would give him a happy, secure life. I was seventeen. And while I had a trust fund, I had no access to it until I was twenty-three."

"And your grandparents wouldn't let you use it? Not even to support your child?"

The judgment in his tone was probably unintended, but she heard it. And was oddly comforted. "Gram was willing to give up the part of it they received for my care. She thought she could talk my dad into giving me more. But it wasn't up to them. My father had full custody of me after my mom died. He set up the trust, with court approval, and he was the executor of it. My grandparents got a monthly stipend for my care, but that came from my father, not from the trust. He also helped pay for any house repairs or other unexpected expenses that came up for them."

Dad was a decent guy. He'd just eventually made a different life for himself. One that hadn't fit her. And he'd been kind enough to facilitate her need to stay in Marie Cove.

Life wasn't always neatly tied up in a pretty bow.

With his hand on her stomach, the telling seemed almost natural. Two boy babies. One in the now. One in the past.

But connected within her.

"So you went to your father for guidance, and he basically forced you to give up the baby."

She'd been an unwed teenage mother. The situation had been of her own making. The consequences of a completely thoughtless and selfish choice. His defense of her...

She had no idea what to do with it.

Gram and Gramps hadn't blamed her. They'd told

her over and over that she needn't feel shame. That her heart was good and pure. She'd loved Nathan with all her heart, and that wasn't a bad thing. They'd all loved him.

"Tammy, my stepmother, offered to keep him, to raise him," she said, hearing her voice as though it belonged to someone else in the darkened vehicle. "She cried with me…"

Her throat tightened and tears sprang behind her lids. She pushed against them. Waited until she'd won the once-familiar battle.

"My dad said no. He felt that it would hold me back. That I'd never have closure. He also didn't think it would be fair to Ryder, being raised by his grandparents with his mother in and out of his life. Or, an alternative, to lie to him about his parentage. He said that it would be kinder to give the baby a family that was ready to love and raise him. And kinder to me to put the pregnancy behind me and move forward with my life. To give me a fresh start. To that end, he purposely arranged a private adoption so that I'd have no chance of contact, forcing me to let go."

She'd been forced to move on. And was only these last months realizing that a mother never let go. Or, at least, she hadn't.

And couldn't. Not completely. She'd always love the baby she'd never known. Always wonder if he was okay...happy...loved. If he knew he was adopted...

"And you started a business whose emphasis is on open fertility donations, focusing not only on the parents' rights, but on the rights of those who contribute," Jamie said.

She shrugged. Life taught you lessons and if you wanted to be happy, you used them for good.

"But you know his name. Ryder."

Shaking her head, she stopped when the movement affected Jamie's hand on his baby. "That's just what I called him. To myself." She didn't like how pathetic that made her sound. She wasn't pathetic at all. She was a strong woman with a great life that she loved.

"So..." He moved his hand and she stiffened, expecting him to take away his warmth, and relaxed when he settled his palm on the left side of her stomach. Then his fingers moved slightly, adding a little pressure, as though playing with his son, and a fissure passed through her. Lighting up her body. "What happened to the father?"

She should have expected the question. Hadn't. Nathan wasn't part of a baby discussion. Wasn't a detail she'd ever have shared with clients in her office.

Weighing the advisability of staying in the SUV with Jamie or going in the house, she searched for words.

"Chris?"

She turned automatically to look at him. Then realized maybe she shouldn't have done so.

"You're sacrificing so much for me, changing my entire world. Please let me give back."

Sirens went off inside her. They didn't come with particular words. Just clear warning. "You're giving me far more than most surrogates get," she said. This was a business deal.

She'd lost sight of the goal. That wasn't good. No way that was good.

"I think you know I'm not talking about money. But what do I get to give for the maternal gift you're bestowing upon my baby?"

She didn't love his baby.

He hadn't said *love*.

"I care about you, Chris. It's ridiculous for us to keep pretending that's not the case. I get that there are boundaries we can't cross, but let me at least be your friend. Accept my gift of caring as I'm accepting yours."

She had friends. A lot of them.

None that had ever called her *Chris*. Not more than once. She always corrected them. Always. She was Christine. All grown-up.

A grown-up could tell a little story from the past.

"His name was Nathan. I met him my senior year. He was a foster kid, also a senior, but new to Marie Cove and the high school so you wouldn't have known him."

Jamie and Emily had gone to USC and hadn't even been in Marie Cove during the year and a half she'd known Nathan and then spent birthing Ryder.

"Nathan was responsible, grounded. More like me than any of the other kids. He knew life's realities and thought of others. Life wasn't just all about him. He wanted to join the military and loved talking to Gramps about Gramps's time in the service. He wanted to spend time with me here, at the house, with my grandparents, and jumped right in and did things for them when he saw a need." Had she reinvented the guy over the years? Romanticized him?

She'd certainly replayed those months over and over and over again. Far too many times.

"He told me repeatedly that it was so great to be part of a real family. When I got pregnant a few months before graduation, I was scared, of course, upset with us for not being more careful, but I was also kind of excited. I figured life was going to be different than I'd thought, but still be great for all of us. Until he balked. He didn't want a baby. Didn't want me to have it. Didn't want to have anything to do with it. He'd been planning to see the world. Was just biding his time until he turned eighteen and could get out of Marie Cove and start living. His whole plan to join the military was so that he could travel to faraway places. He turned eighteen a couple of weeks before the end of the school year and left town the day after graduation without even saying goodbye."

There. She'd given Jamie what he wanted.

His hand moved. Or the baby did. And the next thing she knew, she was sobbing. Big, gross, childish sobs all over the man who'd somehow found a way past the thirteen years' worth of thickening walls protecting her heart.

Chapter Nineteen

Sliding his hand from Chris's belly to her back happened naturally. Jamie didn't consider options or consequences. The second she broke, he had her, pulling her to him, cradling her head against his shoulder. He was no psychiatrist or trained counselor, but he'd seen this one coming.

There was nothing to say, no words that were going to help. He could only sit with her. Share her pain as best he could.

He'd known his own kind of grief. Sometimes being with another while the onslaught raged was just better than being alone.

Time passed; he wasn't counting it.

The neighborhood around them was quiet, unaware of the storm inside their cocoon of darkness. At one point as she sniffled, he leaned over enough to grab some napkins out of the glove box, handed them to her and then wrapped his arm right back around her. Shielding her from the outside world just long enough for her to purge some of the pain trapped inside her.

And feeling some of that pain. At first, when his throat tightened, he didn't get what was happening. But as his gaze on the street outside started to glisten, he recognized the sorrow gathering up inside him. Not for him. Not for Emily or their losses. But for Chris.

All for her.

"I'm so sorry." She didn't pull away as her sobs eased. Just lay against him for the moment. He wanted to be her support for as long as she needed him.

"Don't be. Please, don't ever look back on this moment with remorse," he told her softly.

She turned her head to look up at him, her eyes raised in question, and he lifted his thumb to the tears on her cheeks, wiping them away as though he could somehow take away the pain that had caused them.

He couldn't return her to thirteen years in the past. Couldn't reverse choices or return her son to her.

She continued to hold his gaze, letting him see the woman behind the mask, while he gently brushed her skin. She was so ungodly beautiful he ached with it.

Drawing his thumb down the trail of her tears, he ended up at the corner of her mouth. Gently moving from her mouth, over an inch and down, to return and repeat the gesture.

There was no motive anymore. No forethought. Just a need to be there, connected to her. Her lips opened when he brought his thumb back to them, only inches away from his own, and he lowered his head.

The kiss was instinctive. A way to bring them closer still, to join their pain, their lives. He didn't ask what he was doing, he just did it. And when her lips opened farther, moving against his, he deepened the touch, opening his mouth fully, finding her tongue with his, melding them. He wasn't going anywhere with any of it. Just living in the moment that was there.

Doing what felt natural. Right.

His arms pulled her closer, cradled her neck, as he broke contact only to deepen it more, to kiss her in a way he didn't know, didn't recognize. Fire burned through him, need so hot it erupted, obliterating any thought he might have had. He had to take them further, go with her into an unknown. His erection straining against his pants, he moved, straining toward her pelvis, her hip. He didn't know until she pressed forward, joining their intimate parts through their clothes, how badly he'd needed his penis to find welcome against her.

"No!" With an emotion-filled cry, she pulled away from him. Her eyes glinted with tears in the street-light as she wiped her mouth. "No," she said, more calmly.

Christine had just entered the vehicle. He didn't have to ask or wonder—he knew.

And instantly respected her right to be there.

Feeling blindsided, like a deer in headlights, he tried to make sense of what had just happened. When what he'd just been denied had him in such a strong-hold he could barely form coherent thought.

"This is wrong."

He didn't deny the point. Couldn't. He had no frame of reference for what he'd just experienced. It didn't feel wrong. But it made no sense, and in his world if it didn't make sense, there was some-thing wrong.

But…

"Caring about someone isn't wrong," he said. "Chris" almost slipped out of his mouth. He refused "Christine." "Being present when someone is hurting is one of the purest forms of expressing humanity."

Where in hell were the words coming from? Cer-tainly no math equation.

Her nod was the first thing that had made any sense to him since he'd been brushing a tear off a cheek.

"The kiss," she said. "It's wrong and it can't hap-pen again. If you even try, I'll have to enforce the

clause in our contract that states that I can, with
cause, refuse to see you, which would deny you access to your son until his birth."

He heard the words, saw her hand reach for the
door.

"It won't happen again." He wasn't going to lose
her. Or these months with his son.

She nodded. Pulled up on the door handle.

"But, just for the record, it wasn't all me."

His parting shot was cheap.

But it was also the truth.

The consequences of sexual passion had almost
ruined her life once. Almost killed her, if she were
honest and considered the darkest hours just after
she'd given birth to Ryder. They'd given her something to help her sleep and for a moment there, as
she'd been drifting off, she hadn't wanted to wake up.

Falling for the notion that she had a good partner
who would hold her when she had a weak moment
had been the catalyst that led her to having sex with
Nathan. They'd only done it once. It hadn't been
planned. She'd been crying because her grandfather
had had a dizzy spell and had fallen that day. She'd
seen it happen, been unable to help him.

The doctor had said he'd be fine. They'd only
kept him in the hospital overnight as a precaution.
Gram, of course, had insisted on staying with him.
As was right.

And Christine had been home alone, reliving the moment. Coming face-to-face with the proof that the source of her strength was getting weaker.

That Gramps wouldn't be around forever.

When Nathan called and she told him what happened, he'd come right over. Had held her as she'd cried…

She'd thought he was the real thing. Her soul mate. The man she'd been meant to find. The "Gramps" to her "Gram."

Then she'd grown up.

That first night after Jamie had kissed her, she'd taken a hot bath and had gone to bed. Determined to be kind to herself, and others. To get up in the morning and go to work. To help others have children to feed.

She didn't sleep all that well.

By noon the next day, she couldn't sit still and pushed Jamie's speed dial on her cell phone. If work, helping others, wasn't sufficient, she'd done something wrong.

She knew she had.

"I'm so glad you called," he said, picking up on the first ring. She'd waited until his lunch break from class. It would have been wrong to do otherwise. She knew his schedule. "I apologize profusely, Christine. I can guarantee you it won't happen again."

It sounded as though he'd rehearsed the words.

Or listened to them repeating in his brain too many times for too many hours.

"Christine." Thank God he'd reverted.

And to the sadness within her at the loss of his "Chris," she told herself to grow a pair.

"I'm calling to apologize for my overreaction last night," she said, hearing the stiffness in her voice and finding that a good thing. "I realize I am as much or more to blame as you were and that it was wrong and weak of me to threaten you with the 'cause' clause."

Silence hung on the line and she took advantage of it. "That said, there cannot be a repeat of last night. Not any of it. We have an emotional project going on here. It was bound to bring forth intense feelings in both of us. But we're aware now. We're adults. And I have complete faith that we can both handle this."

He answered immediately. "I agree. I'm embarrassed, ashamed, and I do apologize. You were having a low moment and I pushed my way in to a space in which I didn't belong. It won't happen again."

His tone, the distance and sincerity, spoke volumes. Grateful that the call had gone better than she'd imagined it could, she hung up.

And started to cry.

"I wanted to have sex with him." The words flew out of Christine's mouth the second Olivia slid into the booth that night at a pub they often frequented. Christine had been facilitating a women's health class early that evening, with the volunteered help from Cheryl Miller, but had called Olivia to ask if her friend could do a late dinner.

"Did you?" Olivia hadn't even put her purse on the seat beside her. It hung suspended in air, as her friend looked over at her.

"Want to? Yes."

"No, did you do it?"

Would Olivia be disappointed in her if she had?

"Of course not."

"But you wanted to." Purse on the seat beside her, Olivia leaned forward, her hands folded on the table.

She'd just said she had. What more did the woman want?

Orange and black garlands hung between their booth and the ones behind them on each side. Streamed mellow pop music played softly in the background, and the staff was all wearing spider antler headbands. Christine had helped the staff decorate the clinic for Halloween, but she hadn't even so much as put up a Christmas tree at home since Gram had died.

"So, why didn't you?"

"You know why! It would have been completely unethical! Unprofessional!"

When Olivia nodded, she calmed. And added, "And because I'm not going to make the mistake of letting a man comfort me into sex twice."

She knew, when she said the words, what she was

doing. Opening the door to the question she'd known Olivia would ask…

"There was a first time?"

And it all came out. The waiter came to take their order. Olivia asked for more time without interruption. Christine was aware, but didn't get involved. And as soon as the young man was out of earshot, continued with her story. All of it. Every single detail she could remember.

At some point Olivia ordered club sandwiches for both of them. Christine ate every bite. She had a baby to feed.

And when she was done with her story, she felt physically full, and otherwise, no better. If anything, she felt worse. Weak. Like a victim instead of the survivor she was.

She pulled out her wallet to pay and get the hell out of there. She needed rest.

Olivia's hand covered hers on the little tray holding their bill. "Whoa, wait, what are you doing?"

"I'm paying," she said firmly. "I asked for this dinner. I spent the whole time whining. I'm paying."

"We aren't done yet."

Christine frowned. Looked across at her friend. "We can be done."

Shaking her head, Olivia asked, "Why did you tell me all of this?"

Yeah, it had been a mistake. They'd been friends for years and didn't spill beans that had long since been consumed. "I'm sorry. I know it's not like me. All I can do is play the hormone card and get this baby birthed." She still had a little over four months to go. Tried to chuckle.

An image of Jamie, his face so close it seemed like she could read words in his eyes, sprang to mind.

And she longed for him. Right then. Right there. Longed to be near him. To hear his voice. To kiss him again and not stop.

She was birthing the baby he'd created with another woman. A baby they had created out of deep and abiding love for each other.

What in the hell was the matter with her?

"No, seriously." Olivia's tone was soft, soothing. "Why did you tell me this?"

She didn't know. Wished she hadn't. She shook her head. Wanted to go. And to stay.

"It wasn't right, sweetie, what they did to you back then. A teenager, being left to care for aging grandparents. Not only taking on the day-to-day responsibility, but bearing the weight of it in the bigger picture. It might have been what you thought you wanted, but they were adults—they should have known better…"

"It was my home. Is still my home. I love it there." And truly couldn't imagine wanting to live anywhere else.

"So maybe someone else should have borne the

responsibility of their health so that you could live there and still be a kid."

Maybe. But like she'd told Jamie, life wasn't always neat and perfect.

"Taking care of them… I love that about me. I don't resent one single second of it."

"You don't regret not getting to sit in the lunchroom with friends and be privy to the gossip? Or to try out for cheerleading or band? You must have been lonely. Didn't you ever wish it could have happened differently?"

Of course she had. The loneliness had been acute. Which was why she'd been so ripe for Nathan's support and companionship. "They couldn't help getting sick," she said. "Just like Mom couldn't help dying in childbirth, trying to give me the sibling I wanted. Or like any of your patients can't help getting diseases that end up requiring great sacrifice of, and pain to, their parents."

"So if you weren't looking for a clearer understanding of the past, why did you bring it all up now?" Olivia's glance was serious. Firm.

"Because you and I are the same," she said. "Because you get that a woman can choose to give her life to a career and others, and have that life be as valuable, as happy, as one who chooses not to live alone."

Olivia's gaze darkened. "Oh, sweetie," she said.

Appeared to have some difficulty swallowing. "We aren't alike at all in one very important way…"

Their waiter came close, looking at them, and turned away.

"Yes, I believe a woman dedicating herself to her career can be vital, but that's very different from choosing to be alone. You can be all those things you described and still share your life."

Christine opened her mouth to argue. Figured she'd said enough. Until you'd lived without any freedom because you were tied to loved ones, because you were all they had, because they meant so much to you, you probably wouldn't understand.

"Nine years ago, when I was still in med school, I was married." Olivia's words shocked her. Olivia had been *married*? "My husband was ten years older than me, and wanted to have children right away. He was also quite wealthy and thought it made more sense for us to start our family, and *then* for me to go to med school. It was our only real issue—my dedication to a career—and I adored him. We compromised—we'd start our family, but I was also going to stay in school. Our baby was born with severe birth defects. She lived almost four months, but then we lost her." Olivia's tone didn't change. She was speaking facts, not feeling the emotions they created. Christine knew because she recognized herself in her friend.

"Don't tell me the jerk blamed you…because you were in school or something…"

"No." Olivia's smile was tinged with sadness. "And he wasn't a jerk. But Lily's death was hard on our marriage. I ended up specializing in pediatrics and buried myself in saving other people's children. The last straw for us was when we found out I couldn't have any more babies." Olivia explained that the problem was not with her eggs, but in her body's inability to successfully nourish a fetus.

"I admire the hell out of what you're doing here," she said, leaning in with arms crossed on the table in front of her as she spoke to Christine. There were other people around, parties coming and going, but Christine had hardly been aware of anyone. "Giving a man a chance to have his child…it's incredible. Being able to have a child at all is an incredible thing to me…"

So they weren't alike. Something awakened in Christine. She couldn't define it. Didn't recognize it. But felt enlightened just the same.

"But I'm telling you this because I'm not alone by choice, Christine. I adored my husband when I married him. And I adore him still. He's a good man. A great man. We just weren't good together after Lily died. We handled it differently. I needed to work. To bury myself alive or die of grief. He needed more of me. More from me. You know the statistics…how many marriages fail when a couple loses a child. It doesn't kill the love, though. And I haven't met a man who even comes close to instilling that kind of love or passion in me."

"Do you ever see him?"

"Sometimes. Not often. It's too hard." She waved her hand and then leaned in again. "When I asked you why you didn't sleep with Jamie, you immediately spouted off about professional ethics," she said. "But those are only going to be an issue until after the baby's born."

Tension passed through her system. Grabbing hold.

"I'm thinking there might be more to it than that. You didn't need to speak to me, someone who you thought was like you, if your only concern was professionalism," Olivia continued, and Christine felt like a woman tied to a train track with an engine veering down on her.

She needed to stop her friend before she said anything else. And needed to hear what was being said, too. Olivia was right. She'd told her about her past for a reason.

Because it seemed to be looming in her present, and she couldn't put it to rest. From the time she'd graduated from college and opened the clinic, she'd never looked back. Never had a problem leaving the past behind. She'd been happy.

Content. At peace.

"Is it possible that you've been hiding behind professionalism all these years, finding enough satisfaction in The Parent Portal and the family you've built there to keep from being hurt again?"

"Of course not." She was a woman with her eyes wide-open. Had been since the moment she'd given birth and allowed the nurse to take her child away and never bring him back.

Sitting back, Olivia reached for her purse. "Okay," she said. "It was just a thought. So, if your only problem is the professional relationship between you and Jamie, the solution is simple. Wait it out until you recover from having the baby and then sleep with him."

No. She frowned, putting her credit card on the tray with the bill. No, she was not going to sleep with Jamison Howe.

"I'm having his wife's baby. She's the one he loves. I'm just a stand-in."

"Maybe." She seemed to be waiting for more.

"The last time I felt this way, my heart broke."

Olivia just nodded with her whole upper body, back and forth.

And the peace in Christine's heart shattered, engulfing her with fear.

She'd believed in happily-ever-after once. Had given her whole heart to her mom and dad, her grandparents, Nathan. Ryder. And had it shattered. Again. And again. And again. And once more after that.

She'd survived. And other than her mother's death, she'd handled it all alone.

She couldn't do it again. Couldn't open herself up to another possible loss.

She just couldn't.

Chapter Twenty

Jamie went running first thing Saturday morning. In athletic shorts and a long-sleeved T-shirt, he put on his newest tennis shoes and took off down the beach from his little cottage. He'd spoken to Christine twice since their Wednesday night skitter off course. Normally he'd have requested to visit with her.

He didn't.

He missed his baby like crazy.

Missed Christine almost as badly.

Felt like he'd been unfaithful to his wife. To her memory. Kissing the woman who was carrying Emily's child.

Even wanting to kiss her.

Wanting to make love to her with a fire that burned hotter than anything he'd ever felt before. The truth poured through him as he ran, consuming him with shame.

He couldn't hide from what had happened. Or how he'd felt.

Didn't even attempt to try.

He just didn't know how he could come to terms with either Christine or his son, feeling as he did.

Half an hour into the run he came face-to-face with waves slapping up against a cliffside at the beach's end. He could turn around. Head back. Or go up and over, with the hope that he'd be able to reach sand on the other side. The shoreline had more beach. For more than a hundred miles. He just had no idea what cliffs came in between sandy stretches.

Feeling as though his whole life was suddenly filled with unknowns, unable to tolerate not knowing what lay ahead, he started to climb. Slid a couple of times, scraping his arm pretty badly, bruising a knee, but he kept going, and twenty minutes in, saw a way that would have been quicker. And saw beach, too. As soon as his shoes hit sand, he started running again. Only briefly availing himself of the waterspout attached to the pack on his back.

Em?

Where was she?

Where was *he*?

Why didn't he feel even the slightest bit of resentment that Christine was carrying the child Emily had been meant to carry? She'd assumed, near the beginning of the pregnancy, that he would resent her.

And the house… He couldn't wait to get out of the house he and Emily had bought together. The home she'd loved. Yet, here he was, still just looking at homes like he had all the time in the world, feeling no rush to find a new one, happy in his little cottage.

He'd been told the owners were willing to sell, and he'd actually been thinking about buying it. It would be great for a weekend at the beach. For his and Tom's visitors. Or for his mother to stay in when she visited.

But if he wasn't in a hurry to get into the new house, why rush out of the old? He'd told Christine that it hadn't ever felt like a home to him. And felt badly afterward.

But the words were true.

He wanted their child, but not the home Emily had created for it?

Sand flew behind him as he ran on mostly deserted land. If he got to a public beach, there'd be a few people milling about. There always were, no matter what time of year.

Emily had loved the beach best in nonsummer times. She'd liked the brisk air. The fact that people weren't there to worship the sun, but the water.

The house—there'd been no passion there. He'd always thought, once he and Emily finally bought their "forever" home, it would automatically warm with their love in every room.

He'd wanted the type of intensity he'd witnessed between his parents anytime they'd been in the same room in their home.

Because at home they could let down all barriers and just be completely themselves.

The apartments he'd shared with Emily had all been owned by others, and they could hear others through the walls. But their own home...

He ran as though angry with the sand. Barely aware of the water off to the left. Or the slight cliff leading to grass and hopes to his right.

Em?

The intensity between his parents...

It reminded him of the other night in the car with Christine...

He stopped. Bent over, his hands on his knees, gasping for air.

Shook himself off. Tried to start running again. And fell to his butt in the sand, knees raised, facing the ocean.

He'd loved Emily with all his heart. First as a friend. A best friend. And then forever.

And Christine...

She had brought passion to his life.

She was carrying the baby he'd created with his wife, and he'd fallen in love for the first time in his life.

What in the hell was he going to do with that?

* * *

When Jamie didn't suggest an outing by Sunday afternoon, Christine called him. She'd been completely out of line threatening to enforce her right to not see him for the remainder of the pregnancy.

He must be treading carefully, afraid he'd do something to set her off, and she couldn't have that.

"I have to decide by tomorrow what finish I want on the floors, either just a clear gloss, or tinted coating, and I could sure use some help," she told him about her renovations, including the fact that she was being mindful of chemicals that could affect the baby, keeping things just as they'd been before the night of the show. They'd meet up in the midst of normal life, and then go on with their separate lives.

When he didn't immediately respond in the affirmative, she added, "He's been kicking up a storm all weekend. He needs to hear your voice."

The baby was his. She couldn't fall in love with it. Which meant that he had to cover that part.

So, they'd kissed.

And she'd cried. She was pregnant. She was allowed to be out of her head a bit. Once the baby was born, her hormones leveled out, she'd be happy with her life again.

And even if Olivia *was* somewhat right about some things, Christine had already made her choices. Luckily she'd had warning to guard herself against

Jamie before she'd done something really stupid like fall in love with him.

That's all the kiss had been. A warning to herself.

She'd dressed in a baggy denim dress with colorful flowered lace trim, and as soon as he stood, in jeans and a short-sleeved polo shirt in her living room, his hazel eyes assessing her in a way that felt far too personal, like he knew her too well, she started to panic. And quickly calmed herself with the knowledge that fear was a warning and she was taking heed.

"It's good to see you," she said, to put him at ease. To let him know that nothing had changed between them.

He smiled. "It's good to see you, too." His words were warm. And that gaze… It was like he was leaning in to kiss her without moving. So she turned away.

Cut off anything that might be misconstrued or cause trouble.

She walked through the downstairs, which was all hardwood. Showed him sample colors. Didn't give an opinion. And he chose the clear gloss—her own first pick.

Then it was time for him to go. Except that he asked what she was doing with the upstairs.

"Nothing. It's all carpet and I don't know if I'll have enough to do the whole place this year." Which wasn't really the case. With what he was paying her, she'd have plenty to do both. But she'd been thinking about new tubs and showers. And she wanted to put some of the money away. Maybe invest it.

A girl could never be too sure of her future.

When he asked to take a look, she took him upstairs. Waited in the hall at each door as he peeked inside.

"This place is a castle," he said, as he glanced into the master suite she'd moved into after opening The Parent Portal. Her grandparents had moved back into it after her father moved out. And they'd been gone, within months of each other, since her sophomore year of college.

There were five bedrooms in all. "You can just hear all the kids making noise up here," he said.

And she started downstairs. "There's never been more than just one," she told him, shutting down the picture he'd painted before it could take on color. "My grands bought it from a couple who'd been in the movie business in LA and had it built to have a place to entertain quietly, outside the city." She turned around and grinned at him, holding on to the handrail as she traversed the steps with her bigger belly. "In other words, so they could entertain without everyone who was someone knowing who they were with." They'd reached the first floor and she moved toward the front door. "And then Gram and Gramps only had Mom, and she only had me," she finished, efficiently obliterating any idea of those upstairs rooms filled with noisy kids.

"Don't you get lonely here all alone?"

"Nope." It was home. Filled with all the love she'd ever known.

The baby moved as she reached for the door handle, and pulling back, she said, "He's kicking," and turned her stomach toward him. The baby was his purpose for being there.

Jamie's hand connected with her stomach immediately, no hesitation, and while she braced herself to remain immune, to take herself out of the picture, she also relaxed into his touch. This was them.

She was good.

"I've decided on a name for him," he said.

She nodded. None of her business.

"I figure, if he can hear us talking, he might as well start learning it."

Made sense. Good sense. She looked up at him.

"I'm going to call him Will, after my father." She smiled. "And Ryder, after your son. To honor what you're doing for us."

William Ryder Howe.

Her smile faltered. She teared up. Put some kind of "you don't have to" sentence together. Suggested naming the baby for Emily's father, or to at least think about it.

And when he hugged her goodbye, holding his

baby close to his stomach through her skin, she hugged him back.

Then made herself let go.

Jamie couldn't push her to admit it—if he did, he'd push her away. But after that Sunday visit, the couple that followed that week, a quick stop in her office and a toned-down game of racquetball, he was fairly certain that Christine had feelings for him.

The truth came not so much in the things she said, but in the sometimes stilted, almost rehearsed, way she said them. The careful way she guided their times together—not at all the naturally compassionate professional he'd once known. In the memory of the hunger in her kiss. New to passion as he was, there was no doubting that she'd been as hot for him as he'd been for her. The truth came to him through her eyes when she'd meet his gaze and say nothing at all.

The truth was more than just an awareness of her attraction to him. Her caring about him. Unless something changed for her, she wasn't going to be able to open her heart enough to love anyone intimately. She'd given all she had.

Unless he found a way to show her that she didn't have to go through life, or bear life's challenges, alone.

And the only way he could figure out to show her that, to prove it to her, because telling certainly wasn't going to do it, was to do for her the one thing that mattered most. And that she deemed impossible.

He had to find her son, Ryder. Or at least do all he could to try. To see if there was any way he could at least give her some peace of mind about the child's welfare.

It was a tall order for anyone, let alone a guy who had no rights in her private life at all.

Over the next couple of weeks, he alternated between searching keywords on the internet and telling himself to stop being a fool and get on with his life.

He called a couple of old friends from high school who'd been younger than him, ones he hadn't spoken to in years, shared the news of his impending fatherhood, and, when congratulations were done, he'd caught up on their lives and then awkward silences had fallen on the line when he'd asked about a girl who'd gone to high school with them. Nobody remembered Christine.

He saw her three times a week, both of those weeks, including a routine doctor's visit, and all six times, he came home more determined that he had to find her son. For every pound she gained she grew more vulnerable. More fragile. And more determined than ever that when the baby was born, their lives would return to normal.

And while his would be a brand-new normal, hers would be the normal she knew.

He could touch her stomach. He could even hug

her goodbye fairly regularly. But he absolutely could not talk about any kind of future that included her postbirth. There were times when he caught her looking wistfully at her own stomach. When she asked about his house search and worried that he wouldn't get in in time for the baby to have a nursery. Times when he knew she was hurting. But she played her part without fail.

She'd let him in once. It was clear she wouldn't do so again.

Christine Elliott was a strong woman. She knew what she knew. Believed what life had taught her. And was true to herself.

He'd never met anyone who really believed, to their core, that they could, and should, go it alone. Nor one who would be so incredibly great at more. So ultimately happy.

How he knew that, he didn't question.

He just knew that Ryder was the key to helping her find the happiness she deserved. The key to unlocking her heart so that she could let herself be loved. By him or not. At that point, it didn't even matter who she loved, only that she knew she could. She'd never believe she wasn't alone when alone was all she knew. All she felt.

He had to find her son.

Desperation had a way of pushing a guy forward even when the order was too tall, it seemed. That was the only reason he could give himself for the fact that three and a half weeks after he'd felt bone-deep burning passion for the first time in his life, Jamie was in Los Angeles, waiting to be shown into the office of a man he'd never met.

Playing scenarios through his mind. Did he introduce himself as the father of the baby his daughter was carrying?

In some scenarios that seemed the most powerful way to go. And in others, it was far too messy. For all he knew her father wasn't happy about her choice, would resent Jamie, which would make the trip another lost cause.

A hugely disappointing one. He was out of ideas.

"Dr. Howe? Mr. Elliott will see you now."

The financial manager, dressed impeccably in a gray suit with white shirt and sedate silk tie, stood from behind his desk as Jamie, feeling decidedly underdressed in the brown pants, beige short-sleeved shirt and tie he'd worn to class in Mission Viejo that day, entered the room with a confidence that wilted with every step.

He didn't let it show, though. He'd learned from the best over the past few months how to be who you had to be, regardless of the personal toll.

"I understand you insisted on speaking with me personally," Dennis Elliott said. He had graying short hair, but his dark eyes were exactly like his daughter's. He didn't hold out a hand. Jamie didn't offer one. Nor did he sit down. And Jamie followed suit.

"Yes, sir. I…"

"I think I can save us both some time here. While the firm is always happy to take on new clients, my book is completely full. I can, however, give you a personal reference to the broker who's been with me the longest. I'm happy to show you his portfolio, that which isn't confidential, to give you an idea of his accomplishments and capabilities."

Jamie wasn't the least bit deterred. If anything he'd gained strength with every word the man said. How dare he leave his little girl's heart to just suffocate and die?

The anger that assailed him came as much of a surprise as had the passion in his SUV weeks ago. And the jitters that had assailed him at his first meeting with Christine more than five months before. Maybe he'd always been a calm man because he'd never loved as fiercely as Christine had loved others all of her life.

"I'm not here to make either of us money," he said. Dennis Elliott could very well be a wonderful husband and father, a great man, but, standing there, Jamie resented the hell out of the man who'd chosen making money over being there for his daughter. Who'd assuaged his own grief rather than helping his daughter pick up the pieces of her shattered life.

Again and again.

"I'm a…friend…of your daughter's." Not rehearsed rhetoric. He had no idea if Elliott would pick up his phone the second Jamie left the room and get his daughter on the phone. If he was, in essence, putting the nails on his own coffin.

He only knew that, even if he was, he had to do it. He had to show Christine that someone would move mountains to try and be there for her.

And with that thought, the way became completely, calmly, clear to him. "In fact, sir, I am in love with her. Completely."

The man sat. "Christine's in love?"

Was there relief mixed in with the incredulity in the man's tone? Jamie couldn't take the time to find out. Or allow the distraction.

"I want to marry her," he said, as though the idea had been consciously in his mind when he'd walked in that door.

He hadn't even thought about marriage. Maybe he should have. Emily would be shaking her head with that grin of hers and teasing him about his emotional denseness.

The thought of his wife didn't bring shame. Strangely, the memory of that grin comforted him.

"I don't know a thing about you, but if you managed to get past Christine's independence, then you have my full support," Dennis said. "I can't tell you how…"

"Sir, if I may…" Jamie interrupted, his tone filled with the confidence of the man in charge of a class filled with exceptionally smart people. "I've come

seeking your help. You mention Christine's independence, but it's more than that. Her independence
masks pain that was too much for her to bear. I think
it stems from losing her mother and son."

He sounded like some kind of therapist. Funny,
how smart love made you when you cared enough
to see.

"But…she hasn't mentioned me to you at all, I
take it?" Dennis asked.

"No, she has not."

Had she mentioned the pregnancy? Surely her father knew…

"When was the last time you saw her?"

"Several months ago. Christine's like that. We'd
love to see her more, but we generally have to settle
for once or twice a year."

Good to know. He was betting the man didn't even
know his daughter was pregnant again. Which made
him all that much more determined to be successful
in his quest. At whatever cost to Dennis Elliott. Or
himself, for that matter.

"I believe Christine loves me, but she won't listen to her heart," Jamie said. "All that's ever done
has brought her pain. Hurt her. And she won't let
herself need anyone. Or believe that anyone can be
there for her."

When the man nodded, eyeing him with fingers
steepled at his lips, Jamie continued.

"I need to find her son, sir." Jamie held up a hand

when the man opened his mouth. "I understand that the adoption was closed. I also understand you handled all of the details. I'm not asking for the impossible here." Okay, maybe he was. So be it. "I understand that you might not know who the parents are, and even if you do, you have no way of forcing whoever adopted her son to allow her to see him. I'm just asking you for any information you can give me, the name of the agency through which we could request someone contact the parents. We don't need a picture. Or to know where he is. We don't even need a name. If I could just let her know that he's okay. That he's loved and happy…"

He was a man in love. Fighting for the woman he loved. Not for himself. But for her.

Even if she hated him for doing what he was doing, if he could give her back even a hope of opening her life to love again—any kind of love. Partner. Parent…

"Her whole life, her family, is that clinic—where she makes sure, every day, that no biological parent, or child, under her jurisdiction, and in conjunction with the law, is ever prevented from knowing of one another. Her whole life, sir. She gets up every day to make sure that in her little part of the world, no one suffers as she does. Every day."

Dennis Elliott stood. Sat on the corner of his desk.

"What do you do?" he asked, studying Jamie. "For a living?"

Jamie might have been more put off by the question, in response to his plea, if he hadn't spent the past several months with Christine. In at least one way she appeared to have learned from her father to avoid internal emotional warfare by changing the subject to something innocuous. He knew the drill.

"I'm a college professor. Mathematics." Sweating, Jamie was inordinately thankful he'd opted not to mention that he was also the father of Christine's surrogate child. Or even that she was carrying a child.

"Where do you teach?" Jamie named the university branch in Mission Viejo and the college in Marie Cove.

Dennis nodded. "You're local a lot of the time, then."

"I am."

"You own a home?"

"I did. I sold it." And then he added, "I'm making an offer on the little cottage on the beach I'm renting until I find something. It'll be nice to have for romantic weekends, or summer days at the beach. And for out-of-town guests."

He hadn't even told Christine his plan, and he was telling her father?

"She'd love that. But, you know, she'll never leave that house she's in."

He nodded. "I think part of my problem finding a house is that none of them measure up to that one.

I've never been in a building that feels so much like home."

"So she hasn't asked you to live with her?"

He didn't answer. But his gaze didn't back down at all.

"She doesn't know I'm here, sir, and might never speak to me again when she finds out." A bit of an exaggeration. He hoped. Though, technically, she didn't need to say anything to him during doctor's appointments and the birth.

Dennis wiped a hand slowly down his face. Glanced at a picture on his desk. Jamie could only see an angled back of the frame. Wondered if Christine was in it. Or if it was just his current wife and son.

"I can't promise anything. I'll have to make a call. But I know who adopted Chris's baby."

Chapter Twenty-One

Chris wasn't all that happy about going with Jamie to Anaheim, over an hour's drive from Marie Cove, one Saturday in her sixth month of pregnancy. She'd put him off the first time he'd asked her to accompany him to see the same group of students who'd performed in Mission Viejo be guest artists on the main stage at Disneyland. But when he'd asked a second time, saying he wanted to support his students, but really didn't want to show up to the busy park alone and then added that it would be good for the baby to hear his voice in a crowd of voices, she reluctantly gave in.

She wore yoga pants, a long, colorful, tight-fitting tunic top and tennis shoes without socks and was kind of looking forward to the day as she climbed into Jamie's SUV and strapped herself into that so comfortable seat.

But she dialed her enthusiasm down the second he smiled at her. In jeans and a T-shirt, with his dark hair curling at the collar, he definitely needed to be some woman's husband. Her stomach warmed, her heart pounded harder and she knew the fear was her mind's way of telling her to be careful. To guard herself. It wasn't like she'd be getting much out of the theme park anyway. They weren't staying long and she couldn't do many of the attractions due to her condition.

And the last time she and Jamie had taken a trip out of Marie Cove—the only other time they'd been in a vehicle together—had nearly ended their relationship.

It had thrown her life in a quandary that she didn't care to repeat.

"I talked to my mom today," Jamie said as he set the cruise control for highway driving. "She's planning to stay a month after Will's born."

"That gives you three months to find a house or you'll be sleeping on a very big couch in a very little room." His little rental had two bedrooms, but from what he'd said, one was nearly full with baby stuff already.

Not her business.

"I bought the cottage."

Turning to look at him, determining that he wasn't kidding, she didn't try to hide her shock. "Why? That place isn't big enough to raise a child. Besides, it's too close to the water. A toddler learns how to open doors anywhere from eighteen months to two years, depending on his height and it only takes a second with your head turned…"

When she heard the vehemence in a statement she had no business making, she cut herself off. Stared straight ahead.

And realized her hand was cradling her baby bump. She snatched it away. But it was *her* stomach and where else was she going to put her hand? She tried the door handle. Around her belly to her thigh. The edge of the seat beside her thigh. And back to her belly.

Then, at Jamie's silence, turned to see him alternately watching her and the road. Back and forth.

She wasn't saying another word.

"I'm hoping to be in a new house by the time Mom comes," he said. "And she can use the cottage. It can be a weekend fun spot, you know, for days at the beach. And a place for Mom to stay. My house won't ever be big enough for me to have her watching over my shoulder like she's done ever since my father died."

"I'm sure it's just because she loves you and knows the pain of loss…"

He glanced at her again, and she swore she

wouldn't take her gaze off the road in front of them for the rest of the day. "I'm sure you're right," was all he said.

His mother had lost her husband. Her father had lost his wife. Each parent had a child, about the same age, at home.

She hadn't ever put the facts together quite like that. Realizing that she and Jamie had something kind of deep in common. He'd had Emily's parents watching out for him. She'd had Gram and Gramps. Both of their single parents had remarried, but there'd been one major difference. Jamie's mother had kept him with them.

Thinking of which brought back to mind her father's odd phone call a few days before. Him calling every month or so to check in, if she hadn't called him or Tammy, was normal enough. But before he'd hung up, he'd told her he loved her. Out of the blue, just said the words.

She hadn't known what to do with them. Had pretended she hadn't heard. She couldn't remember the last time he'd expressed any deep emotion around her, and he chose then, when she was hormonal and not herself?

Not that he'd know that. She'd purposely chosen not to tell him about her surrogacy. Just hadn't wanted to go there. It meant she was going to have to make up some kind of excuse to miss Christmas dinner, but she could always say she was volunteering over the holiday. He'd believe that.

Jamie streamed music most of the way, mellow country mostly, and she put her seat back and napped a little bit. She didn't remember being as tired when she'd been pregnant before, but it wasn't like she'd spent a lot of time hanging on to, or cataloging those memories.

They got stuck in some traffic heading off the freeway and into Anaheim. He kept watching the clock to the point that she said, "We're going to be fine, Jamie. It's still an hour before they're due to go on. We've already got our tickets so we'll be able to go right in…"

"It's like getting on a plane now," he said, more tense then she'd ever seen him. "You have to go through security and have bags checked."

"We've still got plenty of time. Even if we have to park far out in the lot, they have shuttles still, I'm sure… And even if we're a minute or two late, it's not like they're going to know. I'm sure that it will mean the world to them just to see you there afterward…"

His impatience was almost comical—except that it wasn't kind to take pleasure in another's discomfort. He didn't swear, or suddenly start to drive erratically, but he definitely wasn't her Jamie.

No.

Not *her* Jamie. Just the Jamie she was usually with. And really, what did she know? They saw each other a few minutes or a little more, a few times a week. And at the doctor's office, where she was merely a conduit, and he and the doctor were the people with roles to play.

As she'd known would be the case, they were inside the park, heading from the locker area up front, past the first couple of stores—or that last chance to buy souvenirs if you were on your way out—toward Main Street, with almost half an hour to spare.

Excitement lit inside her, on a small scale, as she looked around at the fantasy town where everything was colorful and beautiful and perfect looking. "It looks pretty much like I remember it," she said, smiling at Jamie, who was keeping close beside her. "How can that be?"

The place was crowded, of course, and he seemed more intent on watching out for her than giving any hint of enjoying his surroundings.

Like, at any moment, someone might bump into her stomach and hurt her.

Or the baby. It was about him, not her, she reminded herself.

He knew right where the main stage was and didn't let her veer off course even long enough to take a peek at a couple of Disney characters dressed up for photo ops.

"I have a picture someplace of me and Mom and Dad here," she told him. She'd forgotten that she had it. Figured it was probably in the photo trunk in the attic. She was going to look when she got home. Get it out.

Those were the types of photos that she should frame and put on the hallway walls upstairs—after she got them repainted.

She figured they'd find a seat in the back of the arena, leaving lower seats for guests there to see the whole show, but Jamie led them straight to the front row.

"We're going to block the view of those kids." She leaned over to whisper, getting a whiff of his musky cologne in the process. The scent that seduced her that night in his SUV. She pointed to the bleacher two up behind them.

With a nod, he scooted a couple of feet. But stayed right there in front. Like he thought his students would be looking for him and he wanted to make certain they saw him easily. She hadn't realized how close he was with them. They'd really seemed kind of formal with him when they'd been to their last show.

An emcee came out. Asked the crowd if they'd enjoyed the break. Said he hoped they'd had enough time to get refreshments from the carts she and Jamie had passed on the way in. Jamie scooted closer to her. Put an arm behind her, touching her back, but resting on the metal bench on the far side of her.

No one was going to bump her from behind. And she had support for a back that was starting to ache now and then. So thoughtful.

"Up next in our competition is a thirteen-year-old from Santa Barbara," the emcee said. "Shawn Bretton."

"Competition?" she asked Jamie, looking at her watch, as the audience clapped. "I thought there was a show due to start. Your kids are up in ten minutes."

"This is the show they're in," he said, staring at the stage, his voice a little short. "It's a music competition put on in conjunction with schools and talent agencies."

A young man had walked out onstage dressed in black pants and a white button-down shirt with the sleeve cuffs rolled halfway up his arms. He walked with confidence and stood a bit awkwardly. A combination of adult and kid.

"Tell us a little about yourself, Shawn."

"I'm a student at Shelby Junior High, in the eighth grade. I play baseball, and I hope to study law."

"And what are you going to sing for us today?"

"A song my dad wrote when I was little…"

"Your dad. He's a songwriter?"

"Yeah, but he told me not to say any more about that. I'm me, not him. But can I say one thing?"

"Of course."

"My dad, he's like this man that…" The boy stopped. Pulled the mic he'd walked out with away from his mouth. Looked off in the distance, and then pulled the mic back. "He used to sing. Until the car accident that killed my sister and hurt my dad so he couldn't sing anymore. My mom was hurt, too, and couldn't have any more kids. My dad wrote this song about how life is hard, and it's beautiful, too. It's kind of about our family…"

The kid was so…real. So… She didn't know what. He was cute as could be with dark hair and eyes. She was close enough she could see the expression in those eyes as he glanced down at the first row just before he started to sing.

And the words—about the joy a little boy brings to a family. From his first grin, his first tooth, his first step. How all the firsts teach his parents that everything will be okay as long as they don't let death win. No matter what the future holds, there will always be a first grin, a first tooth, a first step that will bring joy. Because while death was a part of living, so was birth. New life. First grins, first teeth, first steps.

As the boy's perfect high pitch, not yet deepened with puberty, drew to its final close, Christine became aware of herself sitting there. Mesmerized.

And sobbing. With Jamie's arm wrapped tightly around her.

The crowd gave the boy a full second of reverent silence and then exploded into applause around them. Christine sat there, unable to do anything but feel.

How could a child bring such truth to her world? And slap her at the same time?

She'd lost so much. But not a child to death. Her

child lived somewhere. And she hadn't lost her ability to carry a child, as Olivia had.

But had she, in her pain, robbed herself of first grins? First teeth? First steps? Had she robbed herself of the joy of new life because of her loss? Was she letting death win?

"I have to tell you something. Right now," Jamie said, suddenly, looking from his phone, which had signaled a text, to somewhere off to the side of them, and back to her. "And I think you're going to want to hold yourself together."

Of course. That she could do. With a sniffle and a deep breath, she sat up straighter. She was there for him. For his students. He must have seen them off to the side of them. Ready to go on.

Jamie's hand squeezed her shoulder, pulling her so tightly against him she could feel his heart beating. "Shawn Bretton is your son, Chris. And I was under the impression that while you could watch him, you weren't going to get to meet him. His parents offered him the opportunity to meet his birth mother and he chose not to do so. But his parents told me he'd be here today and invited you to come watch him, just not meet him. But I just had a text that his parents saw you sitting here and they're willing to introduce you to him. He just can't know who you are. Anywhere else it would be hard to explain, but here, you could just be a fan of his song."

She heard the words. Listened hard inside her

brain and heard them again. Still reeling from the music, she started to shake. Looked off to the side where Jamie had looked, saw a couple standing there, looking toward her and toward the back of the stage as well.

The boy on the stage. The love. The voice. He played baseball.

And… He was *hers*?

Not hers, but he was who Ryder had become?

She stared into Jamie's eyes. "You found my son?" The words stuck in her throat. Came out in mostly a whisper that he probably couldn't even hear over the crowd talking around them as they awaited judges' scoring and the next act.

Jamie nodded, but the tears in his eyes were her real answer. "Because you don't have to do it alone, Chris…"

Leaning in, she planted her lips on his. It didn't matter that they were on the front bleacher with a crowd behind them. That her son's parents were watching. That she was in his employ, pregnant with a child he'd created with another woman.

She just didn't have any words to thank him.

Jamie fell in love all over again as he stood with his arm around Chris and watched her smile from ear to ear, as she was introduced to the young man she'd birthed. There was no hint of the emotion that had to be roiling inside her, just a self-conscious wipe of her eyes as she told him what a great job he'd done. And thanked him, too.

"I...lost a baby once," she said. "And until today, when I heard you sing... I've been letting my sadness win...so, thank you." The words explained the sign of tears on her face without, in any way, giving a hint that it had to be taking everything she had not to grab the boy in her arms and not let go.

His parents stood on either side of him. But both of them met her gaze as they thanked her profusely for sharing her story with them.

They were thanking her for a lot more than that.

Jamie knew. And in the car, on the way home, Chris said, "How can I mourn a past that not only gave him a much better life than I could have back then, but gave them back their lives, too?" Her head lying back on the rest, she had a small smile on her face as she turned and looked at him. "I won't ever be able to thank you, Jamie. Not ever."

He didn't say a word, just sped as fast as he could to an exit he knew that took him to a road that led straight to the beach.

"Why are we getting off?" she asked, as he exited the freeway. "Do we need gas?"

He nodded. Shook his head. And drove.

She didn't say a word as he pulled into the partially full parking lot and stopped the SUV. A group of teenagers was unloading a cooler out of a van, heading toward the beach just yards away. The ocean roared to shore and receded in the distance.

Unfastening his seat belt, he reached over to unbuckle hers, and then, leaving the console down between them, said, "You're giving life to my son. So I found yours. You owe me nothing…"

He didn't want her gratitude.

Her lips trembled as she teared up, and he noticed her hand cradle her belly. His son. Who she was caring for so carefully. Because that's what she did. Never asking for any emotional sustenance for herself. Or expecting any.

"I love you, Chris. With every fiber of my soul. That's why I found your son. Not for anything for me, but because it's what I know you needed. That's what love is. And I might not live through the night, or I could live to be a hundred, but I will always be loving you and doing everything in my power, wherever I am, to give you moments of joy. It would mean everything to me if you'd share my life with me, raise my son with me, but if not, I'll still be loving you."

She shook her head, and he closed his eyes as his heart sank. And yet, it didn't sink far. Because he'd done it. He'd given her what she'd needed most. And if that meant she went on and opened her heart to someone else somewhere down the road, then that would be enough.

It would really be enough.

Just like an enduring love minus jitters and emotional intensity had been enough of him for Emily?

When her finger brushed against his mouth, and then up to the corner of his eye, he opened them to see her gazing at him, the look in those brown eyes so filled with emotion they glistened, but not with tears.

"I'm not good at this, Jamie. I want to spend a life with you, to raise this baby with you. I don't even know how to start. All I know is being alone."

With one hand he had the console up and was already reaching for her. "I can be patient," he said, moving over as he pulled her to him, until they were away from the steering wheel and her pregnant self was on his lap. "And I have it on good authority that I'm an excellent teacher," he said, knowing when to give her what she needed. In that moment, she was her father's daughter. Needing a minute of distraction from an intensity she'd forgotten how to trust. To embrace.

"I love you, Jamie Howe."

Her words dropped softly into the vehicle, wrapping around him. Words he hadn't been sure he'd hear. Words he hadn't been sure she'd ever be able to say.

"I love you, too." He didn't bother to try to hide the tremor in his voice. Or the arms that held her.

She nodded. Settled more firmly against him and said, "I want to wait to have sex with you until I'm just me again. I need to know you see me as me, not as his incubator…"

"I've never seen you that way," he interrupted. He'd done his own reading. About transference, too. But he also understood.

Chris was Christine. She needed that part of herself. And more, the world needed her. She had a purpose that served far more than just him.

"I was going to say that as long as you agree that there will be no sex until I've recovered from the birth, then it would probably make sense for you to move out of the cottage and storage and into the home that it looks like we'll be sharing for the rest of our lives…my house."

He chuckled. He couldn't help it. And then laughed out loud. Chris might be coming back to life, but Christine was right there with them. Just getting right down to the practical.

"What?" she asked, pulling back.

"You," he told her, kissing her. Long and deep. Without any humor at all. And yet, he was pulsing with a euphoria all new to him. "If you're okay with it, I'll start moving in tomorrow. And I hope you have a room in mind for William Ryder's nursery because I have a load of boxes to open and furniture to start putting together. Our son's going to be here before we know it." He placed his hand on her belly, and while she placed hers on top of it, she shook her head.

"The next one will be ours, Jamie," she said.

"I will love William Ryder as much, I will mother him with all of my being, but he belongs to you and Emily. When he's old enough to understand, he has to be told. And to honor her."

"I see it a different way," he told her, tracing her lips with his finger. "I see us all back in high school. Emily is my best friend. And you're my girlfriend. And the two of you meet through me, and form your own sisterly closeness. And together, the three of us, go out into the world and support each other throughout our lives, and love each other's children."

"She'll always be a part of us."

"Yes, and you'll always be a part of us, too," he said, not sure how that worked in the real world, but knowing that it all added up to him.

And that his total was right.

"Together. Forever. As a family." Christine's tone was firm.

"Forever." He knew the promise he was making.

And that was real life—and it didn't get better than that.

* * * * *